DOVER · THRIFT · EDITIONS

The Father

AUGUST STRINDBERG

DOVER PUBLICATIONS, INC.
Mineola, New York

DOVER THRIFT EDITIONS

GENERAL EDITOR: PAUL NEGRI

EDITOR OF THIS VOLUME: T. N. R. ROGERS

Copyright

Theatrical Rights

Bibliographical Note

This Dover edition, first published in 2003, contains the unabridged text of Edith and Warner Oland's translation of *The Father* from *August Strindberg: Plays*, published by John W. Luce and Company, Boston, in 1912. The play was first performed and published in Swedish (as *Fadren*) in 1887. We have supplied a new introductory Note for the Dover edition.

Library of Congress Cataloging-in-Publication Data

Strindberg, August, 1849–1912.
  [Fadren. English]
  The Father / August Strindberg.
     p. cm. — (Dover thrift editions)
  ISBN 0-486-43217-3 (pbk.)
   I. Title. II. Series.

PT9812.F3E513 2003
839.72'6—dc21

2003048967

Manufactured in the United States of America
Dover Publications, Inc., 31 East 2nd Street, Mineola, N.Y. 11501

Note

JOHAN AUGUST STRINDBERG (1849–1912), who is honored as the foremost Swedish playwright, is often compared with Henrik Ibsen, the great Norwegian. Ibsen was two decades older, and his plays much more straightforward. "Ibsen's characters think and speak logically and consecutively," wrote Michael Meyer, who translated more than a dozen plays by each man and wrote biographies of both: "Strindberg's dart backwards and forwards. They do not think, or speak, ABCDE but AQBZC." The two men were well aware of each other. Strindberg's earliest successful drama, *Master Olof* (written around 1873), shows Ibsen's influence. And Ibsen, for his part, kept a portrait of Strindberg in his study; he called it "Madness Incipient," and once remarked, "I can't write a line without that madman staring down at me with those crazy eyes."

Strindberg certainly did have a good measure of craziness in his life, but he managed to transform it into art. He was an extraordinarily prolific writer. His published writings in Swedish total fifty-five volumes—novels, poetry, short stories, autobiography, history, and more than seventy plays. He was also a talented painter (his works have fetched record amounts at auctions) and an experimental photographer who attempted to make portraits of people's souls by means of "celestographs" and "crystallizations"—photos made without the use of a lens.

The Father (*Fadren*, 1887), one of his best, most lasting plays, is a powerful, riveting psychological drama that—like many of Strindberg's works—has sometimes been accused of being misogynistic. It certainly focuses, as many of his best writings do, on a battle of the sexes and on what Strindberg sees as the insidious destructive power of women. The father of the title is a retired cavalry captain in a house full of women, a situation he says is like being in a cage full of tigers—"and if I didn't hold a red-hot iron under their noses they would tear me to pieces any moment." But who can reason with tigers? The poor captain lets his guard down a moment, and his destruction is assured.

Many of the torments of Strindberg's own tormented life seem to have focused on women. As the following Biographical Note makes clear, he was one of several children born to a bankrupt aristocrat and a former waitress, who married only shortly before Strindberg's birth. His childhood was painful, poor, and full of tension, and after the death of his mother when he was thirteen, he hated the stepmother his father brought in to take her place.

But if he believed women to be tigers, he still could not live without them. The first of his wives was Siri von Essen, who when he met her in 1875 was married to Baron Wrangel, an officer of the guards. She got a divorce for Strindberg's sake, became an actress (she played the title role in *Miss Julie* in 1889), and married him in 1877 when she was seven months pregnant. (They lost that child, but later had two daughters and a son.) In 1891 he and Siri divorced, and in 1893 he married a young Austrian writer, Frida Uhl. They had a child in 1894 and divorced a year later. When he was fifty he met his third wife—a twenty-two-year-old actress named Harriet Bosse, whom he married in 1901 and soon had another child with. They divorced in 1904 but still slept together occasionally, and Strindberg claimed that he maintained a telepathic communication with her until she remarried. (In the "Occult Diary" he kept from 1896 to 1908, he wrote about the visits he believed he was receiving from her spirit—even as she was preparing to marry another man.)

Strindberg died from stomach cancer in May, 1912, but his theatrical innovations far outlived him. As Michael Billington wrote,[1]

> Strindberg envisioned the kind of theatre we all now recognise: one that banished needless intervals, removed painted props and scenery, simplified mask-like make-up and was based on a collaborative intimacy. [He] also wrote about sex with absolute realism, dramatising the compound of love, hate, fury and desire that characterises random couplings and permanent relationships. If Ibsen caught the tensions of the night before, Strindberg revealed the acrid taste of the morning after. . . . The idea of sex as a battleground and marriage as a lifelong torment is partly what makes Strindberg seem so modern: there is a straight line connecting plays like *The Dance of Death* and *The Father* with Osborne's *Look Back in Anger* and Albee's *Who's Afraid of Virginia Woolf?*

Besides Albee and Osborne, he strongly influenced Eugene O'Neill (who described him as "the precursor of all modernity in our present theater"), Samuel Beckett, the German expressionists, Harold Pinter, the great Swedish filmmaker Ingmar Bergman, and countless others.

---

[1] In *The Guardian*, 15 February 2003.

"On a purely theatrical plane," wrote Jens Bjørneboe,[2] "Strindberg has become an inspiration, where Ibsen has become a burden, an immovable gravestone which preserves that form of theater which Ibsen mastered and therefore wished to keep unchanged. In dramatic world literature Strindberg has many descendants, Ibsen none."

WARNER OLAND, who with his wife (the artist Edith Shearn) in 1912 made this translation of *The Father* and also wrote the Strindberg biography in the following pages, was quite an interesting character in his own right. He was born in Sweden in 1879, came to America with his parents in 1892, and became known to the world not as a translator but as a movie star. From 1915 to 1937 he acted in sixty silent movies and thirty-six sound films, including the very first of the "talkies," *The Jazz Singer,* in which he played Cantor Rabinowitz (the father of the character played by Al Jolson). But he was best known as Charlie Chan. He portrayed the Chinese detective in sixteen movies, but in 1937, feeling that his life was being destroyed by alcohol, Oland walked off the set of still another Charlie Chan movie (*Charlie Chan at the Ringside*) and sailed back to Sweden. He died there of pneumonia a year later.

[2]In "Strindberg—den fruktbare," originally published in *Aftenposten,* 4 April 1963; translated from the Norwegian by Esther Greenleaf Mürer.

Contents

Biographical Note[1]

> "I tell you, you must have chaos in you, if you
> would give birth to a dancing star."   *Nietzsche.*

In Stockholm, living almost as a recluse, August Strindberg is dreaming life away. The dancing stars, sprung from the chaos of his being, shine with an ever-increasing refulgence from the high-arched dome of dramatic literature, but he no longer adds to their number. The constellation of the Lion of the North is complete.

At sixty-three, worn by the emotional intensity of a life, into which has been crowded the stress and storm of a universe, he sits at his desk, every day transcribing to his diary a record of those mystical forces which he says regulate his life.

Before him lies a crucifix, hardly as a symbol of sectarian faith, for Strindberg is a Swedenborgian, but a fitting accompaniment, nevertheless, to a state of mind which he expresses in saying, "One gets more and more humble the longer one lives, and in the shadow of death many things look different." A softer light beams from those blue eyes, which, under that tossing crown of tawny hair flung high from a speaking forehead, in times past flashed defiance at every opposition. For him the fierce, unyielding, never-ceasing, ever-pressing strife of mind and unrest of life is passing, an eddy in the tide has borne him into quieter waters, and if the hum of the world reaches his solitude, it no longer rouses him to headlong action.

Secure in his position as the foremost man of letters Sweden has produced in modern times, the last representative of that distinguished group of Scandinavian writers which included Ibsen, Björnson and Brandes, with a Continental reputation surpassing that of any one of them, Strindberg well may be entitled to dream of the past.

One day when in the evolution of the drama Strindberg's technique

---

[1]This Note, by Edith and Warner Oland, the translators, served as the introduction to their 1912 collection, *August Strindberg: Plays.*

shall have served its purpose and, like Ibsen's, be forced to give way before the advance of younger artists, when his most radical views shall have become the commonplaces of pseudo-culture, the scientific psychologist will take the man in hand and, from the minute record of his life, emotions, thoughts, fancies, speculations and nightmares, which he has embodied in autobiographical novels and that most remarkable perhaps of all his creations, abysmal in its pessimism, *The Inferno*, will be drawn a true conception of the man.

That the individual will prove quite as interesting a study as his literary work, even the briefest outline of Strindberg's life will suggest.

The lack of harmony in his soul that has permeated his life and work with theses and antitheses Strindberg tries to explain through heredity, a by no means satisfying or complete solution for the motivation of his frequently unusual conduct and exceptional temperamental qualities, which the abnormal psychologist is in the habit of associating with that not inconsiderable group of cases in which the emotional and temperamental characteristics of the opposite sex are dominant in the individual. His ancestry has been traced back to the sixteenth century, when his father's family was of the titled aristocracy, later, generation after generation, becoming churchmen, although Strindberg's father, Carl Oscar, undertook a commercial career. His mother, Ulrica Eleonora Norling, was the daughter of a poor tailor, whom Strindberg's father first met as a waitress in a hotel, and, falling in love with her, married, after she had borne him three children.

August, christened Johan August, the fourth child, was born at Stockholm, January 22, 1849, soon after his father had become a bankrupt. There was little light or cheer in the boy's home; the misfortune that overtook the family at the time of August's birth always hung over them like a dark cloud; the mother became nervous and worn from the twelve childbirths she survived, the father serious and reserved. The children were brought up strictly and, as August was no favorite, loneliness and hostility filled even his earliest years.

His first school days were spent among boys of the better class, who turned up their noses at his leather breeches and heavy boots. He was taken away from that school and sent where there was a lower class of boys, whose leader he soon became, but in his studies he was far from precocious, though not dull.

As he grew up the family fortunes bettered, and he attended a private school patronized by cultivated and wealthy people. Mixing so with both classes meant much in the development of the youth, and he began to realize that he belonged to both and neither, felt homeless, torn in his sympathies and antipathies, plebian and aristocratic at the same time. In his thirteenth year, his mother died, a loss for which his father was apparently soon consoled, as in less than a year he married his housekeeper. This was another blow to the boy, for he disliked the woman, and there was soon war between them.

At fifteen he fell in love with a woman of thirty of very religious character, and as this was a period of fervent belief with the youth himself, she became an influence in his life for some time, but one day a young comrade asked him to luncheon at a cafe, and for the first time Strindberg partook of schnaps and ale with a hearty meal. This little luncheon was the event which broke up the melancholy introspection of his youth and stirred him to activity.

He went to Uppsala University for one term and then left, partly on account of the lack of funds for books, and partly because the slow, pedantic methods of learning were distasteful to his restless, active nature. He then became a school teacher; next interested in medical science, which he studied energetically, until the realities of suffering drove him from it. About this time, the same time, by the way, that Ibsen's *The League of Youth* was being hissed down at Christiania, the creative artist in Strindberg began to stir, and after six months more of turmoil of soul, he turned to the stage as a possible solution, making his debut at the Dramatiska Theatre in 1869 in Björnson's *Mary Stuart*, in the part of a lord with one line to speak. After two months of no advancement he found courage to ask to be heard in one of the classical roles he had been studying.

The director, tired from a long rehearsal, reluctantly consented to listen to him, likewise, the bored company of actors. Strindberg went on "to do or die," and was soon shouting like a revivalist, and made such a bad impression that he was advised to go to the dramatic school to study. He went home disgusted and heartsick, and, determined to take his life, swallowed an opium pill which he had long been keeping for that purpose.

However, it was not sufficiently powerful, and, a friend coming to see him, he was persuaded to go out, and together they drowned his chagrin in an evening at a café.

The day after was a memorable one, for it was Strindberg's birthday as a dramatist. He was lying on a sofa at home, his body still hot from the shame of his defeat—and wine—trying to figure out how he could persuade his stepmother to effect a reconciliation between him and his father. He saw the scenes played as clearly as though on a stage, and with his brain working at high pressure, in two hours had the scheme for two acts of a comedy worked out. In four days it was finished— Strindberg's first play! It was refused production, but he was complimented, and felt that his honor was saved.

The fever of writing took possession of him and within two months he had finished two comedies, and a tragedy in verse called *Hermione*, which was later produced. Giving so much promise as a dramatist he was persuaded to leave the stage and, unwilling of spirit, returned to Upsala in the spring of 1870, as he was advised that he would never be recognized as a writer unless he had secured a university degree. The means with which to continue his studies were derived from the two hundred crowns left him by his mother, which he now forced his father to allow him to use. Despite this, however, his fortunes often ran to the lowest ebb.

One day Strindberg announced that he had a one act play called *In Rome* to read to the "Runa" (Song) Club, a group of six students whom he had gotten together, and which was devoted exclusively to the reading of the poetry of its members. The play, based upon an incident in the life of Thorvaldsen, was received enthusiastically by the "Runa," and the rest of the night was spent in high talk of Strindberg's future over a champagne supper in his honor given by one of the well-to-do members. These days of homage and appreciation from this student group Strindberg cherishes as the happiest time in his life, but notwithstanding their worshipful attitude, he himself was full of doubts and misgivings about his abilities.

One of these friends sent the manuscript of *In Rome* to the Dramatiska Theatre at Stockholm, where it was accepted and produced anonymously in August of the same year, 1870. Strindberg was present at the première and although it was well received, to him it was all a fine occasion—except the play! He was ashamed of his self-confession in it and fled before the final curtain. He soon finished another play, *The Outlaw*. In this drama, which retains a high place among his plays, Strindberg shows for the first time his lion's claw and in it began to speak with his own voice. It was accepted by the Court Theatre at Stockholm for production during the next autumn, that of 1871.

At the close of the summer, after a violent quarrel with his father, he returned to the university in the hope of finding help from his comrades. Arrived at Upsala, with just one crown, he found that many of his old and more prosperous friends were no longer there. Times were harder than ever.

But at last a gleam of hope came with the news that *The Outlaw* was actually to be produced. And his wildest dreams were then realized, for, despite the unappreciative attitude of the critics toward this splendid viking piece, the king, Carl XV, after seeing the play, commanded Strindberg to appear before him. Strindberg regarded the summons as the perpetration of a practical joke, and only obeyed it after making sure by telegraph that it was not a hoax.

Strindberg tells of the kindly old king standing with a big pipe in his hand as the young author strode between chamberlains and other court dignitaries into the royal presence.

The king, a grandson of Napoleon's marshal Bernadotte and, as a Frenchman on the throne of Sweden, diplomatic enough to desire at least the appearance of being more Swedish than the Swedes, spoke of the pleasure the ancient viking spirit of *The Outlaw* had given him, and, after talking genially for some time, said, "You are the son of Strindberg, the steamship agent, I believe, and so, of course, are not in need."

"Quite the reverse," Strindberg replied, explaining that his father no longer gave him the meager help in his university course, which he had formerly done.

"How much can you get along on per annum until you graduate?" asked the king.

Strindberg was unable to say in a moment. "I'm rather short of coin myself," said the king quite frankly, "but do you think you could manage on eight hundred riksdaler a year?" Strindberg was overwhelmed by such munificence, and the interview was concluded by his introduction to the court treasurer, from whom he received his first quarter's allowance of two hundred crowns.

Full of thankfulness for this unexpected turn of fate, the young dramatist returned to Uppsala. For once he appeared satisfied with his lot, and took up his studies with more earnestness than ever. The year 1871 closed brilliantly for the young writer, for in addition to the kingly favor he received honorable mention from the Swedish Academy for his Greek drama *Hermione*. The following year, 1872, life at the university again began to pall on his restless mind, and he took to painting.

Then followed a serious disagreement with one of the professors, so that when he received word from the court treasurer that it was uncertain whether his stipend could be continued on account of the death of the king, he decided to leave the university for good. At a farewell banquet in his honor, he expressed his appreciation of all he had received from his student friends, saying, "A personality does not develop from itself, but out of each soul it comes in contact with, it sucks a drop, just as the bee gathers its honey from a million flowers giving it forth eventually as its own."

Strindberg went to Stockholm to become a litterateur and, if possible, a creative artist. He gleaned a living from newspaper work for a few months, but in the summer went to a fishing village on a remote island in Bothnia Bay where, in his twenty-third year, he wrote his great historical drama *Master Olof*. Breaking away from traditions and making flesh and blood creations instead of historical skeletons in this play, it was refused by all the managers of the theatres, who assured Strindberg that the public would not tolerate any such unfamiliar methods. Strindberg protested, and defended and tried to elucidate his realistic handling of the almost sacred historical personages, but in vain, for *Master Olof* was not produced until seven years later, when it was put on at the Swedish Theatre at Stockholm in 1880, the year Ibsen was writing *Ghosts* at Sorrento.

In 1874, after a year or two of unsuccessful effort to make a living in various employments, he became assistant at the court library, which was indeed a haven of refuge, a position providing both leisure for study and an assured income. Finding in the library some Chinese parchments which had not been catalogued, he plunged into the study of that language. A treatise which he wrote on the subject won him medals from various learned societies at home, as well as recognition from the French Institute. This success induced the many other treatises that followed, for which he received a variety of decorations, and along with the honors nearly brought upon himself "a salubrious idiocy," to use his own phrase.

Then something happened that stirred the old higher voice in him—he fell in love. He had been invited through a woman friend to go to the home of Baron Wrangel, where his name as an author was esteemed. He refused the invitation, but the next day, walking in the city streets with this same woman friend, they encountered the Baroness Wrangel to whom Strindberg was introduced. The baroness asked him once more to come. He promised to do so, and they separated. As Strindberg's friend went into a shop, he turned to look down the street; noting the beautiful lines of the disappearing figure of the baroness, noting, too, a stray lock of her golden hair, that had escaped from her veil, and played against the white ruching at her throat. He gazed after her long, in fact, until she disappeared in the crowded street. From that moment he was not a free man. The friendship which followed resulted in the divorce of the baroness from her husband and her marriage to Strindberg, December 30, 1877, when he was twenty-eight years old. At last Strindberg had someone to love, to take care of, to worship. This experience of happiness, so strange to him, revived the creative impulse.

The following year, 1878, *Master Olof* was finally accepted for publication, and won immediate praise and appreciation. This, to his mind, belated success, roused in Strindberg a smoldering resentment, which lack of confidence and authority of position and heretofore caused him to repress. He broke out with a burning satire, in novel form, called *The Red Room*, the motto of which he made Voltaire's words "Rien est si désagreable que d'être pendu obscurément."

Hardly more than mention can be made of the important work of this dramatist, poet, novelist, historian, scientist, and philosopher. In 1883 he left Sweden, as the atmosphere there had become too disagreeable for him through controversy after controversy in which he became involved. He joined a group of painters and writers of all nationalities in a little village in France. There he wrote *La France*, setting forth the relations between France and Sweden in olden times. This was published in Paris and the French government tendered him the decoration of the legion of honor which, however, he refused very politely, explaining that he never wore a frock coat! The episode ends amusingly with the publisher, a Swede, receiving the decoration instead. In 1884 the first volume of his famous short stories, called *Marriages*, appeared. It was aimed at the cult that had sprung up from Ibsen's *A Doll's House*, which was threatening the peace of all households. A few days after the publication of *Marriages* the first edition was literally swallowed up. As the book dealt frankly with the facts of physical sex relations, it was confiscated by the Swedish government a month after its publication, and Strindberg was obliged to go to Stockholm to defend his cause in the courts, which he won, and in another month *Marriages* was again on the market.

The next year, 1885, his *Real Utopias* was written in Switzerland, an attack, in the form of four short stories, on overcivilization, which won him much applause in Germany. He went to Italy as a special correspondent for the *Daily News* of Stockholm.

In 1886 the much anticipated second volume of *Marriages* appeared. These were the short stories, satisfying to the simplest as well as to the most discriminating minds, that attracted Nietzsche's attention to Strindberg. A correspondence sprung up between the two men, referring to which in a letter to Peter Gast, Nietzsche said, "Strindberg has written to me, and for the first time I sense an answering note of universality." The mutual admiration and intellectual sympathies of these two conspicuous creative geniuses has led a number of critics, including Edmund Gosse, into the error of attributing to Nietzsche a dominating influence over Strindberg. It should be remembered, however, that *Countess Julie* and *The Father*, which are cited as the most obvious examples of that supposed influence, were completed before Strindberg's acquaintance with Nietzsche's philosophy, and that among others, the late John Davidson is also charged with having drawn largely from Nietzsche. The fact is that during the last quarter of the nineteenth century, the most original thinkers of many countries were quite independently, though less clearly, evolving the same philosophic principals that the master mind of Nietzsche was radiating in the almost blinding flashes of his genius.

Then came the period during which Strindberg attained the highest
peaks of his work, the years 1886–90, with his autobiography, *The
Servant Woman's Son*, the tragedies *The Father* and *Countess Julie*, the
comedies *Comrades* and *The Stronger*, and the tragicomedies *The
Creditor* and *Simoon*. Of these, *The Father* and *Countess Julie* soon
made Strindberg's name known and honored throughout Europe, except in his home country.

In *The Father* perhaps his biggest vision is felt. It was published in
French soon after it appeared in Sweden, with an introduction by Zola
in which he says, "To be brief, you have written a mighty and captivat-
ing work. It is one of the few dramas that have had the power to stir me
to the depths."

Of his choice of theme in *Countess Julie*, Strindberg says: "When I took
this motive from life, as it was related to me a few years ago, it made a
strong impression on me. I found it suitable for tragedy, and it still makes
a sorrowful impression on me to see an individual to whom happiness has
been allotted go under, much more, to see a line become extinct." And in
defense of his realism he has said further in his preface to *Countess Julie*:
"The theatre has for a long time seemed to me the *Biblia pauperum* in
the fine arts, a bible with pictures for those who can neither read nor write,
and the dramatist is the revivalist, and the revivalist dishes up the ideas of
the day in popular form, so popular that the middle class, of whom the
bulk of theatre-goers is comprised, can without burdening their brains understand what it is all about. The theatre therefore has always been a
grammar school for the young, the half-educated, and women, who still
possess the primitive power of being able to delude themselves and of allowing themselves to be deluded, that is to say, receive illusions and ac-
cept suggestions from the dramatist. . . . Some people have accused my
tragedy *The Father* of being too sad, as though one desired a merry tragedy.
People call authoritatively for the 'Joy of Life' and theatrical managers call
for farces, as though the Joy of Life lay in being foolish, and in describing
people who each and every one are suffering from St. Vitus' dance or idiocy. I find the joy of life in the powerful, terrible struggles of life; and the
capability of experiencing something, of learning something, is a pleasure
to me. And therefore I have chosen an unusual but instructive subject; in
other words, an exception, but a great exception, that will strengthen the
rules which offend the apostle of the commonplace. What will further
create antipathy in some, is the fact that my plan of action is not simple,
and that there is not one view alone to be taken of it. An event in life —
and that is rather a new discovery — is usually occasioned by a series of
more or less deep-seated motifs, but the spectator generally chooses that
one which his power of judgment finds simplest to grasp, or that his gift
of judgment considers the most honorable. For example, someone com-

mits suicide: 'Bad business!' says the citizen; 'Unhappy love!' says the woman; 'Sickness!' says the sick man; 'Disappointed hopes!' the bankrupt. But it may be that none of these reasons is the real one, and that the dead man hid the real one by pretending another that would throw the most favorable light on his memory. . . . In the following drama (*Countess Julie*) I have not sought to do anything new, because that cannot be done, but only to modernize the form according to the requirements I have considered present-day people require."

Following the mighty output of those years, in 1891 Strindberg went out to the islands where he had lived years before, and led a hermit's life. Many of his romantic plays were written there, and much of his time was spent at painting.

In 1892 he was divorced from his wife.

After a few months Strindberg went to Berlin, where he was received with all honors by literary Germany. Richard Dehmel, one of their foremost minstrels, celebrated the event by a poem called "An Immortal—To Germany's Guest." In the shop windows his picture hung alongside that of Bismarck, and at the theatres his plays were being produced. About this time he heard of the commotion that *Countess Julie* had created in Paris, where it had been produced by Antoine. During these victorious times Strindberg met a young Austrian writer, Frida Uhl, to whom he was married in April 1893. Although the literary giant of the hour, he was nevertheless in very straitened pecuniary circumstances, which led to his allowing the publication of *A Fool's Confession*, written in French, and later, without his permission or knowledge, issued in German and Swedish, which entangled him in a lawsuit, as the subject matter contained much of his marital miseries. Interest in chemistry had long been stirring in Strindberg's mind; it now began to deepen. About this time also he passed through that religious crisis which swept artistic Europe, awakened nearly a century after his death by that Swedenborgian poet and artist, William Blake. To this period belongs *To Damascus*, a play of deepest soul probing, which was not finished however until 1904.

Going to Paris in the fall of 1894, to pursue chemical research most seriously, he ran into his own success at the theatres there. *The Creditor* had been produced and Strindberg was induced to undertake the direction of *The Father* at the Théâtre de l'Oeuvre, where it was a tremendous success. A Norwegian correspondent was forced to send word home that with *The Father* Strindberg had overreached Ibsen in Paris, because what it had never been possible to do with an Ibsen play, have a run in Paris, they were now doing with Strindberg. At the same time the Cercle des Escholiers put on *The Link*, the Odéon produced *The Secret of the Guild*, and the Chat Noir *The Keys of Heaven*, and translations of his novels were running in French periodicals. But Strindberg turned his back on all this success and shut himself up in his laboratory to delve into chemistry. This he did with such earnestness that with his discovery of Swedenborg his experimentations and speculations reduced him to a condition of mind that unfitted him for any kind of companionship, so that when his wife left him to go to their child who was ill and far away, he welcomed the complete freedom. Strindberg says of their parting at the railway station that although they smiled and waved to each other as they called out, "Auf wiedersehn," they both knew that they were saying good-bye forever, which proved to be true, as they were divorced a year later. In 1896 he returned to Sweden so broken in health through his tremendous wrestling with the riddle of life that he went into the sanitorium of his friend Dr. Eliasson at Ystad. After two months he was sufficiently restored to go to Austria, at the invitation of his divorced wife's family, to see his child. Then back to Sweden, to Lund, a university town, where he lived solely to absorb Swedenborg. By May of that year he was able to go to work on *The Inferno*, that record of a soul's nightmare, which in all probability will remain unique in the history of literature. Then came the writing of the great historical dramas, then the realistically symbolic plays of Swedenborgian spirit, of which *Easter* is representative, and the most popular.

When *Easter* was produced in Stockholm a young Norwegian, Harriet Bosse, played Eleonora, the psychic, and in 1901 this young actress became Strindberg's wife. This third marriage ended in divorce three years later. In 1906, the actor-manager August Falk produced *Countess Julie* in Stockholm, seventeen years after it had been written. To Strindberg's amazement, it won such tremendous attention that the other theatres became deserted. In consequence of this success an intimate theatre was founded for the production of none but Strindberg's plays.

How he is estimated today in his own country man be judged by the following extract from an article which appeared in a recent issue of the leading periodical of Stockholm:

"For over thirty years he has dissected us from every point of view; during that time his name has always been conspicuous in every bookshop window and his books gradually push out the others from our shelves; every night his plays are produced at the theatres; every conversation turns on him, and his is the name the pigmies quarrel over daily; the cry is heard that he has become hysterical, sentimental, out of his mind, but the next one knows, he is robustness itself, and enduring beyond belief, despite great need, enmity, sorrow. One hour one is angry over some extravagance which he has allowed himself, the next captivated by one of his plays, stirred, melted, strengthened, and uplifted by his sublime genius."

Characters

A Captain of Cavalry
Laura, his wife
Bertha, their daughter
Doctor Östermark
The Pastor
The Nurse
Nöjd
An Orderly

THE FATHER

ACT I

The sitting room at the Captain's. There is a door a little to the right at the back. In the middle of the room, a large, round table strewn with newspapers and magazines. To right a leather-covered sofa and table. In the right-hand corner a private door. At left there is a door leading to the inner room and a desk with a clock on it. Gamebags, guns and other arms hang on the walls. Army coats hang near door at back. On the large table stands a lighted lamp.

CAPTAIN [*rings, an orderly comes in*].

ORDERLY.   Yes, Captain.

CAPTAIN.   Is Nöjd out there?

ORDERLY.   He is waiting for orders in the kitchen.

CAPTAIN.   In the kitchen again, is he? Send him in at once.

ORDERLY.   Yes, Captain.   [*Goes.*]

PASTOR.   What's the matter now?

CAPTAIN.   Oh the rascal has been cutting up with the servant-girl again; he's certainly a bad lot.

PASTOR.   Why, Nöjd got into the same trouble year before last, didn't he?

CAPTAIN.   Yes, you remember? Won't you be good enough to give him a friendly talking to and perhaps you can make some impression on him. I've sworn at him and flogged him, too, but it hasn't had the least effect.

PASTOR.   And so you want me to preach to him? What effect do you suppose the word of God will have on a rough trooper?

CAPTAIN.   Well, it certainly has no effect on me.

PASTOR.   I know that well enough.

CAPTAIN.   Try it on *him*, anyway.

[NÖJD *comes in.*]

1

CAPTAIN. What have you been up to now, Nöjd?

NÖJD. God save you, Captain, but I couldn't talk about it with the Pastor here.

PASTOR. Don't be afraid of me, my boy.

CAPTAIN. You had better confess or you know what will happen.

NÖJD. Well, you see it was like this; we were at a dance at Gabriel's, and then—then Ludwig said—

CAPTAIN. What has Ludwig got to do with it? Stick to the truth.

NÖJD. Yes, and Emma said "Let's go into the barn——"

CAPTAIN. ——Oh, so it was Emma who led you astray, was it?

NÖJD. Well, not far from it. You know that unless the girl is willing nothing ever happens.

CAPTAIN. Never mind all that: Are you the father of the child or not?

NÖJD. Who knows?

CAPTAIN. What's that? Don't you know?

NÖJD. Why no—that is, you can never be sure.

CAPTAIN. Weren't you the only one?

NÖJD. Yes, that time, but you can't be sure for all that.

CAPTAIN. Are you trying to put the blame on Ludwig? Is that what you are up to?

NÖJD. Well, you see it isn't easy to know who is to blame.

CAPTAIN. Yes, but you told Emma you would marry her.

NÖJD. Oh, a fellow's always got to say that—

CAPTAIN [*to* PASTOR]. This is terrible, isn't it?

PASTOR. It's the old story over again. See here, Nöjd, you surely ought to know whether you are the father or not?

NÖJD. Well, of course I was mixed up with the girl—but you know yourself, Pastor, that it needn't amount to anything for all that.

PASTOR. Look here, my lad, we are talking about you now. Surely you won't leave the girl alone with the child. I suppose we can't compel you to marry her, but you should provide for the child—that you shall do!

NÖJD. Well, then, so must Ludwig, too.

CAPTAIN. Then the case must go to the courts. I cannot ferret out the truth of all this, nor is it to my liking. So now be off.

PASTOR. One moment, Nöjd. H'm—don't you think it dishonorable to leave a girl destitute like that with her child? Don't you think so? Don't you see that such conduct—— h'm—— h'm——

NÖJD. Yes, if I only knew for sure that I was father of the child, but you can't be sure of that, Pastor, and I don't see much fun slaving all your life for another man's child. Surely you, Pastor, and the Captain can understand for yourselves.

CAPTAIN. Be off.

NÖJD.   God save you, Captain.   [*Goes.*]

CAPTAIN.   But keep out of the kitchen, you rascal! [*To* PASTOR.] Now, why didn't you get after him?

PASTOR.   What do you mean?

CAPTAIN.   Why, you only sat and mumbled something or other.

PASTOR.   To tell the truth I really don't know what to say. It is a pity about the girl, yes, and a pity about the lad, too. For think if he were not the father. The girl can nurse the child for four months at the orphanage, and then it will be permanently provided for, but it will be different for him. The girl can get a good place afterwards in some respectable family, but the lad's future may be ruined if he is dismissed from the regiment.

CAPTAIN.   Upon my soul I should like to be in the magistrate's shoes and judge this case. The lad is probably not innocent, one can't be sure, but we do know that the girl is guilty, if there is any guilt in the matter.

PASTOR.   Well, well, I judge no one. But what were we talking about when this stupid business interrupted us? It was about Bertha and her confirmation, wasn't it?

CAPTAIN.   Yes, but it was certainly not in particular about her confirmation but about her whole welfare. This house is full of women who all want to have their say about my child. My mother-in-law wants to make a Spiritualist of her. Laura wants her to be an artist; the governess wants her to be a Methodist, old Margret a Baptist, and the servant-girls want her to join the Salvation Army! It won't do to try to make a soul in patches like that. I, who have the chief right to try to form her character, am constantly opposed in my efforts. And that's why I have decided to send her away from home.

PASTOR.   You have too many women trying to run this house.

CAPTAIN.   You're right! It's like going into a cage full of tigers, and if I didn't hold a red-hot iron under their noses they would tear me to pieces any moment. And you laugh, you rascal! Wasn't it enough that I married your sister, without your palming off your old stepmother on me?

PASTOR.   But, good heavens, one can't have stepmothers in one's own house!

CAPTAIN.   No, you think it is better to have mothers-in-law in some one else's house!

PASTOR.   Oh well, we all have some burden in life.

CAPTAIN.   But mine is certainly too heavy. I have my old nurse into the bargain, who treats me as if I ought still to wear a bib. She is a good old soul, to be sure, and she must not be dragged into such talk.

PASTOR. You must keep a tight rein on the women folks. You let them run things too much.

CAPTAIN. Now will you please inform me how I'm to keep order among the women folk?

PASTOR. Laura was brought up with a firm hand, but although she is my own sister. I must admit she *was* pretty troublesome.

CAPTAIN. Laura certainly has her faults, but with her it isn't so serious.

PASTOR. Oh, speak out—I know her.

CAPTAIN. She was brought up with romantic ideas, and it has been hard for her to find herself, but she is my wife——

PASTOR. And because she is your wife she is the best of wives? No, my dear fellow, it is she who really wears on you most.

CAPTAIN. Well, anyway, the whole house is topsy-turvy. Laura won't let Bertha leave her, and I can't allow her to remain in this bedlam.

PASTOR. Oh, so Laura won't? Well, then, I'm afraid you are in for trouble. When she was a child if she set her mind on anything she used to play dead dog till she got it, and then likely as not she would give it back, explaining that it wasn't the thing she wanted, but having her own way.

CAPTAIN. So she was like that even then? H'm—she really gets into such a passion sometimes that I am anxious about her and afraid she is ill.

PASTOR. But what do you want to do with Bertha that is so unpardonable? Can't you compromise?

CAPTAIN. You mustn't think I want to make a prodigy of her or an image of myself. I don't want to be a procurer for my daughter and educate her exclusively for matrimony, for then if she were left unmarried she might have bitter days. On the other hand, I don't want to influence her toward a career that requires a long course of training which would be entirely thrown away if she should marry.

PASTOR. What do you want, then?

CAPTAIN. I want her to be a teacher. If she remains unmarried she will be able to support herself, and at any rate she wouldn't be any worse off than the poor schoolmasters who have to share their salaries with a family. If she marries she can use her knowledge in the education of her children. Am I right?

PASTOR. Quite right. But, on the other hand, hasn't she shown such talent for painting that it would be a great pity to crush it?

CAPTAIN. No! I have shown her sketches to an eminent painter, and he says they are only the kind of thing that can be learned at schools. But then a young fop came here in the summer who, of course, understands the matter much better, and he declared that she had colossal genius, and so that settled it to Laura's satisfaction.

PASTOR. Was he quite taken with Bertha?

CAPTAIN. That goes without saying.

PASTOR. Then God help you, old man, for in that case I see no hope. This is pretty bad—and, of course, Laura has her supporters—in there?

CAPTAIN. Yes, you may be sure of that; the whole house is already up in arms, and, between ourselves, it is not exactly a noble conflict that is being waged from that quarter.

PASTOR. Don't you think I know that?

CAPTAIN. You do?

PASTOR. I do.

CAPTAIN. But the worst of it is, it strikes me that Bertha's future is being decided from spiteful motives. They hint that men better be careful, because women can do this or that now-a-days. All day long, incessantly, it is a conflict between man and woman. Are you going? No, stay for supper. I have no special inducements to offer, but do stay. You know I am expecting the new doctor. Have you seen him?

PASTOR. I caught a glimpse of him as I came along. He looked pleasant and reliable.

CAPTAIN. That's good. Do you think it possible he may become my ally?

PASTOR. Who can tell? It depends on how much he has been among women.

CAPTAIN. But won't you really stay?

PASTOR. No thanks, my dear fellow; I promised to be home for supper, and the wife gets uneasy if I am late.

CAPTAIN. Uneasy? Angry, you mean. Well, as you will. Let me help you with your coat.

PASTOR. It's certainly pretty cold tonight. Thanks. You must take care of your health, Adolf, you seem rather nervous.

CAPTAIN. Nervous?

PASTOR. Yes, you are not really very well.

CAPTAIN. Has Laura put that into your head? She has treated me for the last twenty years as if I were at the point of death.

PASTOR. Laura? No, but you make me uneasy about you. Take care of yourself—that's my advice! Good-bye, old man; but didn't you want to talk about the confirmation?

CAPTAIN. Not at all! I assure you that matter will have to take its course in the ordinary way at the cost of the clerical conscience, for I am neither a believer nor a martyr.

PASTOR.   Good-bye. Love to Laura.   [*Goes.*]

[*The Captain opens his desk and seats himself at it. Takes up account books.*]

CAPTAIN [*figuring*].   Thirty-four—nine, forty-three—seven, eight, fifty-six—

LAURA [*coming in from inner room*].   Will you be kind enough——

CAPTAIN.   Just a moment! Sixty-six—seventy-one, eighty-four, eighty-nine, ninety-two, a hundred. What is it?

LAURA.   Am I disturbing you?

CAPTAIN.   Not at all. Housekeeping money, I suppose?

LAURA.   Yes, housekeeping money.

CAPTAIN.   Put the accounts down there and I will go over them.

LAURA.   The accounts?

CAPTAIN.   Yes.

LAURA.   Am I to keep accounts now?

CAPTAIN.   Of course you are to keep accounts. Our affairs are in a precarious condition, and in case of a liquidation, accounts are necessary, or one is liable to punishment for being careless.

LAURA.   It's not my fault that our affairs are in a precarious condition.

CAPTAIN.   That is exactly what the accounts will decide.

LAURA.   It's not my fault that our tenant doesn't pay.

CAPTAIN.   Who recommended this tenant so warmly? You! Why did you recommend a—good-for-nothing, we'll call him?

LAURA.   But why did you rent to this good-for-nothing?

CAPTAIN.   Because I was not allowed to eat in peace, nor sleep in peace, nor work in peace, till you women got that man here. You wanted him so that your brother might be rid of him, your mother wanted him because I didn't want him, the governess wanted him because he reads his Bible, and old Margret because she had known his grandmother from childhood. That's why he was taken, and if he hadn't been taken, I'd be in a madhouse by now or lying in my grave. However, here is the housekeeping money and your pin money. You may give me the accounts later.

LAURA [*curtsies*].   Thanks so much. Do you too keep an account of what you spend besides the housekeeping money?

CAPTAIN.   That doesn't concern you.

LAURA.   No, that's true—just as little as my child's education concerns me. Have the gentlemen come to a decision after this evening's conference?

CAPTAIN.   I had already come to a decision, and therefore it only remained for me to talk it over with the one friend I and the family have in common. Bertha is to go to boarding school in town, and starts in a fortnight.

LAURA.   To which boarding school, if I may venture to ask?

CAPTAIN.   Professor Säfberg's.

LAURA.   That free thinker!

CAPTAIN.   According to the law, children are to be brought up in their father's faith.

LAURA.   And the mother has no voice in the matter?

CAPTAIN.   None whatever. She has sold her birthright by a legal transaction, and forfeited her rights in return for the man's responsibility of caring for her and her children.

LAURA.   That is to say she has no rights concerning her child.

CAPTAIN.   No, none at all. When once one has sold one's goods, one cannot have them back and still keep the money.

LAURA.   But if both father and mother should agree?

CAPTAIN.   Do you think that could ever happen? I want her to live in town, you want her to stay at home. The arithmetical result would be that she remain at the railway station midway between town and home. This is a knot that cannot be untied, you see.

LAURA.   Then it must be broken. What did Nöjd want here?

CAPTAIN.   That is an official secret.

LAURA.   Which the whole kitchen knows!

CAPTAIN.   Good, then you must know it.

LAURA.   I do know it.

CAPTAIN.   And have your judgment ready-made?

LAURA.   My judgment is the judgment of the law.

CAPTAIN.   But it is not written in the law who the child's father is.

LAURA.   No, but one usually knows that.

CAPTAIN.   Wise minds claim that one can never know.

LAURA.   That's strange. Can't one ever know who the father of a child is?

CAPTAIN.   No; so they claim.

LAURA.   How extraordinary! How can the father have such control over the children then?

CAPTAIN.   He has control only when he has assumed the responsibilities of the child, or has had them forced upon him. But in wedlock, of course, there is no doubt about the fatherhood.

LAURA.   There are no doubts then?

CAPTAIN.   Well, I should hope not.

LAURA.   But if the wife has been unfaithful?

CAPTAIN.   That's another matter. Was there anything else you wanted to say?

LAURA.   Nothing.

CAPTAIN.   Then I shall go up to my room, and perhaps you will be kind enough to let me know when the doctor arrives.

[*Closes desk and rises.*]

LAURA.   Certainly.

[CAPTAIN *goes through the private door right.*]

CAPTAIN.   As soon as he comes. For I don't want to seem rude to him, you understand.   [*Goes.*]

LAURA.   I understand.   [*Looks at the money she holds in her hands.*]

MOTHER-IN-LAW'S VOICE [*within*].   Laura!

LAURA.   Yes.

MOTHER-IN-LAW'S VOICE.   Is my tea ready?

LAURA [*in doorway to inner room*].   In just a moment.

[LAURA *goes toward hall door at back as the orderly opens it.*]

ORDERLY.   Doctor Östermark.

DOCTOR.   Madam!

LAURA [*advances and offers her hand*].   Welcome, Doctor—you are heartily welcome. The Captain is out, but he will be back soon.

DOCTOR.   I hope you will excuse my coming so late, but I have already been called upon to pay some professional visits.

LAURA.   Sit down, won't you?

DOCTOR.   Thank you.

LAURA.   Yes, there is a great deal of illness in the neighborhood just now, but I hope it will agree with you here. For us country people living in such isolation it is of great value to find a doctor who is interested in his patients, and I hear so many nice things of you, Doctor, that I hope the pleasantest relations will exist between us.

DOCTOR.   You are indeed kind, and I hope for your sake my visits to you will not often be caused by necessity. Your family is, I believe, as a rule in good health——

LAURA.   Fortunately we have been spared acute illnesses, but still things are not altogether as they should be.

DOCTOR.   Indeed?

LAURA.   Heaven knows, things are not as might be wished.

DOCTOR.   Really, you alarm me.

LAURA.   There are some circumstances in a family which through honor and conscience one is forced to conceal from the whole world——

DOCTOR.   Excepting the doctor.

LAURA.   Exactly. It is, therefore, my painful duty to tell you the whole truth immediately.

DOCTOR.   Shouldn't we postpone this conference until I have had the honor of being introduced to the Captain?

LAURA.   No! You must hear me before seeing him.

DOCTOR.   It relates to him then?

LAURA.   Yes, to him, my poor, dear husband.

DOCTOR.   You alarm me, indeed, and believe me, I sympathize with your misfortune.

LAURA [*taking out handkerchief*].   My husband's mind is affected. Now you know all, and may judge for yourself when you see him.

DOCTOR.   What do you say? I have read the Captain's excellent treatises on mineralogy with admiration, and have found that they display a clear and powerful intellect.

LAURA.   Really? How happy I should be if we should all prove to be mistaken.

DOCTOR.   But of course it is possible that his mind might be affected in other directions.

LAURA.   That is just what we fear, too. You see he has sometimes the most extraordinary ideas which, of course, one might expect in a learned man, if they did not have a disastrous effect on the welfare of his whole family. For instance, one of his whims is buying all kinds of things.

DOCTOR.   That is serious; but what does he buy?

LAURA.   Whole boxes of books that he never reads.

DOCTOR.   There is nothing strange about a scholar's buying books.

LAURA.   You don't believe what I am saying?

DOCTOR.   Well, Madam, I am convinced that you believe what you are saying.

LAURA.   Tell me, is it reasonable to think that one can see what is happening on another planet by looking through a microscope?

DOCTOR.   Does he say he can do that?

LAURA.   Yes, that's what he says.

DOCTOR.   Through a microscope?

LAURA.   Through a microscope, yes.

DOCTOR.   This is serious, if it is so.

LAURA.   If it is so! Then you have no faith in me, Doctor, and here I sit confiding the family secret to——

DOCTOR.   Indeed, Madam, I am honored by your confidence, but as a physician I must investigate and observe before giving an opinion. Has the Captain ever shown any symptoms of indecision or instability of will?

LAURA.   Has he! We have been married twenty years, and he has never yet made a decision without changing his mind afterward.

DOCTOR.   Is he obstinate?

LAURA.   He always insists on having his own way, but once he has got it he drops the whole matter and asks me to decide.

DOCTOR.   This is serious, and demands close observation. The will, you see, is the mainspring of the mind, and if it is affected the whole mind goes to pieces.

LAURA.   God knows how I have taught myself to humor his wishes through all these long years of trial. Oh, if you knew what a life I have endured with him—if you only knew.

DOCTOR.   Your misfortune touches me deeply, and I promise you to see what can be done. I pity you with all my heart, and I beg you to trust me completely. But after what I have heard I must ask you to avoid suggesting any ideas that might make a deep impression on the patient, for in a weak brain they develop rapidly and quickly turn to monomania or fixed ideas.

LAURA.   You mean to avoid arousing suspicions?

DOCTOR.   Exactly. One can make the insane believe anything, just because they are receptive to everything.

LAURA.   Indeed? Then I understand. Yes—yes. [A *bell rings within.*] Excuse me, my mother wishes to speak to me. One moment—— — Ah, here is Adolf.

[CAPTAIN *comes in through private door.*]

CAPTAIN.   Oh, here already, Doctor? You are very welcome.

DOCTOR.   Captain! It is a very great pleasure to me to make the acquaintance of so celebrated a man of science.

CAPTAIN.   Oh, I beg of you. The duties of service do not allow me to make any very profound investigations, but I believe I am now really on the track of a discovery.

DOCTOR.   Indeed?

CAPTAIN.   You see, I have submitted meteoric stones to spectrum analysis, with the result that I have found carbon, that is to say, a clear trace of organic life. What do you say to that?

DOCTOR.   Can you see that with a microscope?

CAPTAIN.   Lord, no—with the spectroscope.

DOCTOR.   The spectroscope! Pardon. Then you will soon be able to tell us what is happening on Jupiter.

CAPTAIN.   Not what is happening, but what has happened. If only the confounded booksellers in Paris would send me the books; but I believe all the booksellers in the universe have conspired against me. Think of it, for the last two months not a single one has ever answered my communications, neither letters nor abusive telegrams. I shall go mad over it, and I can't imagine what's the matter.

DOCTOR. Oh, I suppose it's the usual carelessness; you mustn't let it vex you so.

CAPTAIN. But the devil of it is I shall not get my treatise done in time, and I know they are working along the same lines in Berlin. But we shouldn't be talking about this—but about you. If you care to live here we have rooms for you in the wing, or perhaps you would rather live in the old quarters?

DOCTOR. Just as you like.

CAPTAIN. No, as you like. Which is it to be?

DOCTOR. You must decide that, Captain.

CAPTAIN. No, it's not for me to decide. You must say which you prefer. I have no preference in the matter, none at all.

DOCTOR. Oh, but I really cannot decide.

CAPTAIN. For heaven's sake, Doctor, say which you prefer. I have no choice in the matter, no opinion, no wishes. Haven't you got character enough to know what you want? Answer me, or I shall be provoked.

DOCTOR. Well, if it rests with me, I prefer to live here.

CAPTAIN. Thank you—forgive me, Doctor, but nothing annoys me so much as to see people undecided about anything. [*Nurse comes in.*] Oh, there you are, Margret. Do you happen to know whether the rooms in the wing are in order for the Doctor?

NURSE. Yes, sir, they are.

CAPTAIN. Very well. Then I won't detain you, Doctor; you must be tired. Good bye, and welcome once more. I shall see you tomorrow, I hope.

DOCTOR. Good evening, Captain.

CAPTAIN. I daresay that my wife explained conditions here to you a little, so that you have some idea how the land lies?

DOCTOR. Yes, your excellent wife has given me a few hints about this and that, such as were necessary to a stranger. Good evening, Captain.

CAPTAIN [*to* NURSE]. What do you want, you old dear? What is it?

NURSE. Now, little Master Adolf, just listen—

CAPTAIN. Yes, Margret, you are the only one I can listen to without having spasms.

NURSE. Now, listen, Mr. Adolf. Don't you think you should go half-way and come to an agreement with Mistress in this fuss over the child? Just think of a mother——

CAPTAIN. Think of a father, Margret.

NURSE. There, there, there. A father has something besides his child, but a mother has nothing but her child.

CAPTAIN. Just so, you old dear. She has only one burden, but I have three, and I have her burden too. Don't you think that I should hold a better position in the world than that of a poor soldier if I had not had her and her child?

NURSE. Well, that isn't what I wanted to talk about.

CAPTAIN. I can well believe that, for you wanted to make it appear that I am in the wrong.

NURSE. Don't you believe, Mr. Adolf, that I wish you well?

CAPTAIN. Yes, dear friend, I do believe it; but you don't know what is for my good. You see it isn't enough for me to have given the child life, I want to give her my soul, too.

NURSE. Such things I don't understand. But I do think that you ought to be able to agree.

CAPTAIN. You are not my friend, Margret.

NURSE. I? Oh, Lord, what are you saying, Mr. Adolf? Do you think I can forget that you were my child when you were little?

CAPTAIN. Well, you dear, have I forgotten it? You have been like a mother to me, and always have stood by me when I had everybody against me, but now, when I really need you, you desert me and go over to the enemy.

NURSE. The enemy!

CAPTAIN. Yes, the enemy! You know well enough how things are in this house! You have seen everything from the beginning.

NURSE. Indeed I have seen! But, God knows, why two people should torment the life out of each other; two people who are otherwise so good and wish all others well. Mistress is never like that to me or to others——

CAPTAIN. Only to me, I know it. But let me tell you, Margret, if you desert me now, you will do wrong. For now they have begun to weave a plot against me, and that doctor is not my friend.

NURSE. Oh, Mr. Adolf, you believe evil about everybody. But you see it's because you haven't the true faith; that's just what it is.

CAPTAIN. Yes, you and the Baptists have found the only true faith. You are indeed lucky!

NURSE. Anyway, I'm not unhappy like you, Mr. Adolf. Humble your heart and you will see that God will make you happy in your love for your neighbor.

CAPTAIN. It's a strange thing that you no sooner speak of God and love than your voice becomes hard and your eyes fill with hate. No, Margret, surely you have not the true faith.

NURSE. Yes, go on being proud and hard in your learning, but it won't amount to much when it comes to the test.

CAPTAIN. How mightily you talk, humble heart. I know very well that knowledge is of no use to you women.

NURSE.   You ought to be ashamed of yourself. But in spite of everything old Margret cares most for her great big boy, and he will
come back to the fold when it's stormy weather.

CAPTAIN.   Margret! Forgive me, but believe me when I say that there
is no one here who wishes me well but you. Help me, for I feel
that something is going to happen here. What it is, I don't know,
but something evil is on the way. [*Scream from within.*] What's
that? Who's that screaming?

[BERTHA *enters from inner room.*]

BERTHA.   Father! Father! Help me; save me.

CAPTAIN.   My dear child, what is it? Speak!

BERTHA.   Help me. She wants to hurt me.

CAPTAIN.   Who wants to hurt you? Tell me! Speak!

BERTHA.   Grandmother! But it's my fault, for I deceived her.

CAPTAIN.   Tell me more.

BERTHA.   Yes, but you mustn't say anything about it. Promise me you
won't.

CAPTAIN.   Tell me what it is then.

[NURSE *goes.*]

BERTHA.   In the evening she generally turns down the lamp and then
she makes me sit at a table holding a pen over a piece of paper.
And then she says that the spirits are to write.

CAPTAIN.   What's all this—and you have never told me about it?

BERTHA.   Forgive me, but I dared not, for Grandmother says the spirits take revenge if one talks about them. And then the pen writes,
but I don't know whether I'm doing it or not. Sometimes it goes
well, but sometimes it won't go at all, and when I am tired nothing comes, but she wants it to come just the same. And tonight
I thought I was writing beautifully, but then grandmother said it
was all from Stagnelius,[1] and that I had deceived her, and then
she got terribly angry.

CAPTAIN.   Do you believe that there are spirits?

BERTHA.   I don't know.

CAPTAIN.   But I know that there are none.

BERTHA.   But Grandmother says that you don't understand, Father,
and that you do much worse things—you who can see to other
planets.

CAPTAIN.   Does she say that! Does she say that? What else does she
say?

[1]Enk Johan Stagnelius (1793–1823) was a Swedish romantic poet.

BERTHA.   She says that you can't work witchery.

CAPTAIN.   I never said that I could. You know what meteoric stones are—stones that fall from other heavenly bodies. I can examine them and learn whether they contain the same elements as our world. That is all I can tell.

BERTHA.   But Grandmother says that there are things that she can see which you cannot see.

CAPTAIN.   Then she lies.

BERTHA.   Grandmother doesn't tell lies.

CAPTAIN.   Why doesn't she?

BERTHA.   Then Mother tells lies too.

CAPTAIN.   H'm!

BERTHA.   And if you say that Mother lies, I can never believe in you again.

CAPTAIN.   I have not said so, and so you must believe in me when I tell you that it is for your future good that you should leave home. Will you? Will you go to town and learn something useful?

BERTHA.   Oh, yes, I should love to go to town, away from here, any-where. If I can only see you sometimes—often. Oh, it is so gloomy and awful in there all the time, like a winter night, but when you come home, Father, it is like a morning in spring when they take off the double windows.

CAPTAIN.   My beloved child! My dear child!

BERTHA.   But, Father, you'll be good to Mother, won't you? She cries so often.

CAPTAIN.   H'm—then you want to go to town?

BERTHA.   Yes, yes.

CAPTAIN.   But if Mother doesn't want you to go?

BERTHA.   But she must let me.

CAPTAIN.   But if she won't?

BERTHA.   Well, then, I don't know what will happen. But she must! She must!

CAPTAIN.   Will you ask her?

BERTHA.   You must ask her very nicely; she wouldn't pay any attention to my asking.

CAPTAIN.   H'm! Now if you wish it, and I wish it, and she doesn't wish it, what shall we do then?

BERTHA.   Oh, then it will all be in a tangle again! Why can't you both——

[LAURA *comes in.*]

LAURA.   Oh, so Bertha is here. Then perhaps we may have her own opinion as the question of her future has to be decided.

CAPTAIN. The child can hardly have any well-grounded opinion about what a young girl's life is likely to be, while we, on the contrary, can more easily estimate what it may be, as we have seen so many young girls grow up.

LAURA. But as we are of different opinions Bertha must be the one to decide.

CAPTAIN. No, I let no one usurp my rights, neither women nor children. Bertha, leave us.

[BERTHA *goes out.*]

LAURA. You were afraid of hearing her opinion, because you thought it would be to my advantage.

CAPTAIN. I know that she wishes to go away from home, but I know also that you possess the power of changing her mind to suit your pleasure.

LAURA. Oh, am I really so powerful?

CAPTAIN. Yes, you have a fiendish power of getting your own way; but so has anyone who does not scruple about the way it is accomplished. How did you get Doctor Norling away, for instance, and how did you get this new doctor here?

LAURA. Yes, how did I manage that?

CAPTAIN. You insulted the other one so much that he left, and made your brother recommend this fellow.

LAURA. Well, that was quite simple and legitimate. Is Bertha to leave home now?

CAPTAIN. Yes, she is to start in a fortnight.

LAURA. That is your decision?

CAPTAIN. Yes.

LAURA. Then I must try to prevent it.

CAPTAIN. You cannot.

LAURA. Can't I? Do you really think I would trust my daughter to wicked people to have her taught that everything her mother has implanted in her child is mere foolishness? Why, afterward she would despise me all the rest of her life!

CAPTAIN. Do you think that a father should allow ignorant and conceited women to teach his daughter that he is a charlatan?

LAURA. It means less to the father.

CAPTAIN. Why so?

LAURA. Because the mother is closer to the child, as it has been discovered that no one can tell for a certainty who the father of a child is.

CAPTAIN. How does that apply to this case?

LAURA. You do not know whether you are Bertha's father or not.

CAPTAIN. I do not know?

LAURA. No; what no one knows, you surely cannot know.

CAPTAIN. Are you joking?

LAURA. No; I am only making use of your own teaching. For that matter, how do you know that I have not been unfaithful to you?

CAPTAIN. I believe you capable of almost anything, but not that, nor that you would talk about it if it were true.

LAURA. Suppose that I was prepared to bear anything, even to being despised and driven out, everything for the sake of being able to keep and control my child, and that I am truthful now when I declare that Bertha is my child, but not yours. Suppose——

CAPTAIN. Stop now!

LAURA. Just suppose this. In that case your power would be at an end.

CAPTAIN. When you had proved that I was not the father.

LAURA. That would not be difficult! Would you like me to do so?

CAPTAIN. Stop!

LAURA. Of course I should only need to declare the name of the real father, give all details of place and time. For instance—when was Bertha born? In the third year of our marriage.

CAPTAIN. Stop now, or else——

LAURA. Or else, what? Shall we stop now? Think carefully about all you do and decide, and whatever you do, don't make yourself ridiculous.

CAPTAIN. I consider all this most lamentable.

LAURA. Which makes you all the more ridiculous.

CAPTAIN. And you?

LAURA. Oh, we women are really too clever.

CAPTAIN. That's why one cannot contend with you.

LAURA. Then why provoke contests with a superior enemy?

CAPTAIN. Superior?

LAURA. Yes, it's queer, but I have never looked at a man without knowing myself to be his superior.

CAPTAIN. Then you shall be made to see your superior for once, so that you shall never forget it.

LAURA. That will be interesting.

NURSE [*comes in*]. Supper is served. Will you come in?

LAURA. Very well.

[CAPTAIN *lingers; sits down with a magazine in an arm chair near table.*]

LAURA. Aren't you coming in to supper?

CAPTAIN. No, thanks. I don't want anything.

LAURA. What, are you annoyed?

CAPTAIN. No, but I am not hungry.

LAURA. Come, or they will ask unnecessary questions—be good now. You won't? Stay there then.   [*Goes.*]

NURSE. Mr. Adolf! What is this all about?

CAPTAIN. I don't know what it is. Can you explain to me why you women treat an old man as if he were a child?

NURSE. I don't understand it, but it must be because all you men, great and small, are women's children, every man of you.

CAPTAIN. But no women are born of men. Yes, but I am Bertha's father. Tell me, Margret, don't you believe it? Don't you?

NURSE. Lord, how silly you are. Of course you are your own child's father. Come and eat now, and don't sit there and sulk. There, there, come now.

CAPTAIN. Get out, woman. To hell with the hags. [*Goes to private door.*] Svärd, Svärd!

[ORDERLY *comes in.*]

ORDERLY. Yes, Captain.

CAPTAIN. Hitch into the covered sleigh at once.

NURSE. Captain, listen to me.

CAPTAIN. Out, woman! At once!

[ORDERLY *goes.*]

NURSE. Good Lord, what's going to happen now.

[CAPTAIN *puts on his cap and coat and prepares to go out.*]

CAPTAIN. Don't expect me home before midnight.   [*Goes.*]

NURSE. Lord preserve us, whatever will be the end of this!

ACT II

The same scene as in previous act. A lighted lamp is on the table; it is night. The DOCTOR *and* LAURA *are discovered at rise of curtain.*

DOCTOR.   From what I gathered during my conversation with him the case is not fully proved to me. In the first place you made a mistake in saying that he had arrived at these astonishing results about other heavenly bodies by means of a microscope. Now that I have learned that it was a spectroscope, he is not only cleared of any suspicion of insanity, but has rendered a great service to science.

LAURA.   Yes, but I never said that.

DOCTOR.   Madam, I made careful notes of our conversation, and I remember that I asked about this very point because I thought I had misunderstood you. One must be very careful in making such accusations when a certificate in lunacy is in question.

LAURA.   A certificate in lunacy?

DOCTOR.   Yes, you must surely know that an insane person loses both civil and family rights.

LAURA.   No, I did not know that.

DOCTOR.   There was another matter that seemed to me suspicious. He spoke of his communications to his booksellers not being answered. Permit me to ask if you, through motives of mistaken kindness, have intercepted them?

LAURA.   Yes, I have. It was my duty to guard the interests of the family, and I could not let him ruin us all without some intervention.

DOCTOR.   Pardon me, but I think you cannot have considered the consequences of such an act. If he discovers your secret interference in his affairs, he will have grounds for suspicions, and they will grow like an avalanche. And besides, in doing this you have thwarted his will and irritated him still more. You must have felt yourself how the mind rebels when one's deepest desires are thwarted and one's will is crossed.

18

LAURA.   Haven't I felt that!

DOCTOR.   Think, then, what he must have gone through.

LAURA [*rising*].   It is midnight and he hasn't come home. Now we may fear the worst.

DOCTOR.   But tell me what actually happened this evening after I left. I must know everything.

LAURA.   He raved in the wildest way and had the strangest ideas. For instance, that he is not the father of his child.

DOCTOR.   That is strange. How did such an idea come into his head?

LAURA.   I really can't imagine, unless it was because he had to question one of the men about supporting a child, and when I tried to defend the girl, he grew excited and said no one could tell who was the father of a child. God knows I did everything to calm him, but now I believe there is no help for him.   [*Cries.*]

DOCTOR.   But this cannot go on. Something must be done here without, of course, arousing his suspicions. Tell me, has the Captain ever had such delusions before?

LAURA.   Six years ago things were in the same state, and then he, himself, confessed in his own letter to the doctor that he feared for his reason.

DOCTOR.   Yes, yes, yes, this is a story that has deep roots and the sanctity of the family life—and so on—of course I cannot ask about everything, but must limit myself to appearances. What is done can't be undone, more's the pity, yet the remedy should be based upon all the past.—Where do you think he is now?

LAURA.   I have no idea, he has such wild streaks.

DOCTOR.   Would you like to have me stay until he returns? To avoid suspicion, I could say that I had come to see your mother who is not well.

LAURA.   Yes, that will do very nicely. Don't leave us, Doctor; if you only knew how troubled I am! But wouldn't it be better to tell him outright what you think of his condition.

DOCTOR.   We never do that unless the patient mentions the subject himself, and very seldom even then. It depends entirely on the case. But we mustn't sit here; perhaps I had better go into the next room; it will look more natural.

LAURA.   Yes, that will be better, and Margret can sit here. She always waits up when he is out, and she is the only one who has any power over him. [*Goes to the door left.*] Margret, Margret!

NURSE.   Yes, Ma'am. Has the master come home?

LAURA.   No; but you are to sit here and wait for him, and when he does come you are to say my mother is ill and that's why the doctor is here.

NURSE.   Yes, yes. I'll see that everything is all right.
LAURA [*Opens the door to inner rooms.*]   Will you come in here, Doctor?
DOCTOR.   Thank you.

[NURSE *seats herself at the table and takes up a hymn book and spectacles and reads.*]

NURSE.   Ah, yes, ah yes!   [*Reads half aloud.*]
        Ah woe is me, how sad a thing
          Is life within this vale of tears,
        Death's angel triumphs like a king,
          And calls aloud to all the spheres—
              Vanity, all is vanity.
Yes, yes! Yes, yes!

                                            [*Reads again.*]
        All that on earth hath life and breath
        To earth must fall before his spear,
        And sorrow, saved alone from death,
        Inscribes above the mighty bier.
              Vanity, all is vanity.
Yes, Yes.

BERTHA [*Comes in with a coffee-pot and some embroidery. She speaks in a low voice.*]   Margret, may I sit with you? It is so frightfully lonely up there.
NURSE.   For goodness sake, are you still up, Bertha?
BERTHA.   You see I want to finish Father's Christmas present. And here's something that you'll like.
NURSE.   But bless my soul, this won't do. You must be up in the morning, and it's after midnight now.
BERTHA.   What does it matter? I don't dare sit up there alone. I believe the spirits are at work.
NURSE.   You see, just what I've said. Mark my words, this house was not built on a lucky spot. What did you hear?
BERTHA.   Think of it, I heard some one singing up in the attic!
NURSE.   In the attic? At this hour?
BERTHA.   Yes, it was such a sorrowful, melancholy song! I never heard anything like it. It sounded as if it came from the store-room, where the cradle stands, you know, to the left——
NURSE.   Dear me, Dear me! And such a fearful night. It seems as if the chimneys would blow down. "Ah, what is then this earthly life, But grief, affliction and great strife? E'en when fairest it has seemed, Nought but pain it can be deemed." Ah, dear child, may God give us a good Christmas!

BERTHA. Margret, is it true that Father is ill?

NURSE. Yes, I'm afraid he is.

BERTHA. Then we can't keep Christmas eve? But how can he be up and around if he is ill?

NURSE. You see, my child, the kind of illness he has doesn't keep him from being up. Hush, there's some one out in the hall. Go to bed now and take the coffee-pot away or the master will be angry.

BERTHA [*Going out with tray.*] Good night, Margret.

NURSE. Good night, my child. God bless you.

[CAPTAIN *comes in, takes off his overcoat.*]

CAPTAIN. Are you still up? Go to bed.

NURSE. I was only waiting till——

[CAPTAIN *lights a candle, opens his desk, sits down at it and takes letters and newspapers out of his pocket.*]

NURSE. Mr. Adolf.

CAPTAIN. What do you want?

NURSE. Old mistress is ill and the doctor is here.

CAPTAIN. Is it anything dangerous?

NURSE. No, I don't think so. Just a cold.

CAPTAIN [*Gets up.*] Margret, who was the father of your child?

NURSE. Oh, I've told you many and many a time; it was that scamp Johansson.

CAPTAIN. Are you sure that it was he?

NURSE. How childish you are; of course I'm sure when he was the only one.

CAPTAIN. Yes, but was he sure that he was the only one? No, he could not be, but you could be sure of it. There is a difference, you see.

NURSE. Well, I can't see any difference.

CAPTAIN. No, you cannot see it, but the difference exists, nevertheless. [*Turns over the pages of a photograph album which is on the table.*] Do you think Bertha looks like me?

NURSE. Of course! Why, you are as like as two peas.

CAPTAIN. Did Johansson confess that he was the father?

NURSE. He was forced to!

CAPTAIN. How terrible! Here is the Doctor.

[DOCTOR *comes in.*]

Good evening, Doctor. How is my mother-in-law?

DOCTOR. Oh, it's nothing serious; merely a slight sprain of the left ankle.

CAPTAIN. I thought Margret said it was a cold. There seem to be different opinions about the same case. Go to bed, Margret.

[NURSE *goes. A pause.*]

CAPTAIN. Sit down, Doctor.

DOCTOR [*sits*]. Thanks.

CAPTAIN. Is it true that you obtain striped foals if you cross a zebra and a mare?

DOCTOR [*astonished*]. Perfectly true.

CAPTAIN. Is it true that the foals continue to be striped if the breed is continued with a stallion?

DOCTOR. Yes, that is true, too.

CAPTAIN. That is to say, under certain conditions a stallion can be sire to striped foals or the opposite?

DOCTOR. Yes, so it seems.

CAPTAIN. Therefore an offspring's likeness to the father proves nothing?

DOCTOR. Well——

CAPTAIN. That is to say, paternity cannot be proven.

DOCTOR. H'm—— well——

CAPTAIN. You are a widower, aren't you, and have had children?

DOCTOR. Ye-es.

CAPTAIN. Didn't you ever feel ridiculous as a father? I know of nothing so ludicrous as to see a father leading his children by the hand around the streets, or to hear a father talk about his children. "My wife's children," he ought to say. Did you ever feel how false your position was? Weren't you ever afflicted with doubts, I won't say suspicions, for, as a gentleman, I assume that your wife was above suspicion.

DOCTOR. No, really, I never was; but, Captain, I believe Goethe says a man must take his children on good faith.

CAPTAIN. It's risky to take anything on good faith where a woman is concerned.

DOCTOR. Oh, there are so many kinds of women.

CAPTAIN. Modern investigations have pronounced that there is only one kind! Lately I have recalled two instances in my life that make me believe this. When I was young I was strong and, if I may boast, handsome. Once when I was making a trip on a steamer and sitting with a few friends in the saloon, the young stewardess came and flung herself down by me, burst into tears, and told us that her sweetheart was drowned. We sympathized with her, and I ordered some champagne. After the second glass I touched her foot; after the fourth her knee, and before morning I had consoled her.

DOCTOR.   That was just a winter fly.

CAPTAIN.   Now comes the second instance—and that was a real summer fly. I was at Lysekil. There was a young married woman stop-
ping there with her children, but her husband was in town. She
was religious, had extremely strict principles, preached morals to
me, and was, I believe, entirely honorable. I lent her a book, two
books, and when she was leaving, she returned them, strange to
say! Three months later, in those very books I found her card with
a declaration on it. It was innocent, as innocent as a declaration of
love can be from a married woman to a strange man who never
made any advances. Now comes the moral. Just don't have too
much faith.

DOCTOR.   Don't have too little faith either.

CAPTAIN.   No, but just enough. But, you see, Doctor, that woman was
so unconsciously dishonest that she talked to her husband about
the fancy she had taken to me. That's what makes it dangerous,
this very unconsciousness of their instinctive dishonesty. That is a
mitigating circumstance, I admit, but it cannot nullify judgment,
only soften it.

DOCTOR.   Captain, your thoughts are taking a morbid turn, and you
ought to control them.

CAPTAIN.   You must not use the word morbid. Steam boilers, as you
know, explode at a certain pressure, but the same pressure is not
needed for all boiler explosions. You understand? However, you
are here to watch me. If I were not a man I should have the
right to make accusations or complaints, as they are so cleverly
called, and perhaps I should be able to give you the whole di-
agnosis, and, what is more, the history of my disease. But unfortunately, I am a man, and there is nothing for me to do but,
like a Roman, fold my arms across my breast and hold my
breath till I die.

DOCTOR.   Captain, if you are ill, it will not reflect upon your honor
as a man to tell me all. In fact, I ought to hear the other side.

CAPTAIN.   You have had enough in hearing the one, I imagine. Do
you know when I heard Mrs. Alving eulogizing her dead husband,
I thought to myself what a damned pity it was the fellow was dead.
Do you suppose that he would have spoken if he had been alive?
And do you suppose that if any of the dead husbands came back
they would be believed? Good night, Doctor. You see that I am
calm, and you can retire without fear.

DOCTOR.   Good night, then, Captain. I'm afraid I can be of no further
use in this case.

CAPTAIN.   Are we enemies?

DOCTOR.   Far from it. But it is too bad we cannot be friends. Good
   night.

   [*Goes. The* CAPTAIN *follows the* DOCTOR *to the door at back and
then goes to the door at left and opens it slightly.*]

CAPTAIN.   Come in, and we'll talk. I heard you out there listening.
   [LAURA, *embarrassed.* CAPTAIN *sits at desk.*] It is late, but we must
   come to some decision. Sit down. [*Pause.*] I have been at the post
   office tonight to get my letters. From these it appears that you have
   been keeping back my mail, both coming and going. The consequence of which is that the loss of time has as good as destroyed
   the result I expected from my work.
LAURA.   It was an act of kindness on my part, as you neglected the service for this other work.
CAPTAIN.   It was hardly kindness, for you were quite sure that some
   day I should win more honor from that than from the service; but
   you were particularly anxious that I should not win such honors,
   for fear your own insignificance would be emphasized by it. In
   consequence of all this I have intercepted letters addressed to you.
LAURA.   That was a noble act.
CAPTAIN.   You see, you have, as you might say, a high opinion of me.
   It appears from these letters that for some time past you have been
   arraying my old friends against me by spreading reports about my
   mental condition. And you have succeeded in your efforts, for
   now not more than one person exists, from the Colonel down to
   the cook, who believes that I am sane. Now these are the facts
   about my illness; my mind is sound, as you know, so that I can take
   care of my duties in the service as well as my responsibilities as a
   father; my feelings are more or less under my control, as my will
   has not been completely undermined; but you have gnawed and
   nibbled at it so that it will soon slip the cogs, and then the whole
   mechanism will slip and go to smash. I will not appeal to your
   feelings, for you have none; that is your strength; but I will appeal
   to your interests.
LAURA.   Let me hear.
CAPTAIN.   You have succeeded in arousing my suspicions to such an
   extent that my judgment is no longer clear, and my thoughts
   begin to wander. This is the approaching insanity that you are
   waiting for, which may come at any time now. So you are face
   to face with the question whether it is more to your interest that
   I should be sane or insane. Consider. If I go under I shall lose
   the service, and where will you be then? If I die, my life insur-
   ance will fall to you. But if I take my own life, you will get

nothing. Consequently, it is to your interest that I should live out my life.

LAURA. Is this a trap?

CAPTAIN. To be sure. But it rests with you whether you will run around it or stick your head into it.

LAURA. You say that you will kill yourself! You won't do that!

CAPTAIN. Are you sure? Do you think a man can live when he has nothing and no one to live for?

LAURA. You surrender, then?

CAPTAIN. No, I offer peace.

LAURA. The conditions?

CAPTAIN. That I may keep my reason. Free me from my suspicions and I give up the conflict.

LAURA. What suspicions?

CAPTAIN. About Bertha's origin.

LAURA. Are there any doubts about that?

CAPTAIN. Yes, I have doubts, and you have awakened them.

LAURA. I?

CAPTAIN. Yes, you have dropped them like henbane in my ears, and circumstances have strengthened them. Free me from the uncertainty; tell me outright that it is true and I will forgive you beforehand.

LAURA. How can I acknowledge a sin that I have not committed?

CAPTAIN. What does it matter when you know that I shall not divulge it? Do you think a man would go and spread his own shame broadcast?

LAURA. If I say it isn't true, you won't be convinced; but if I say it is, then you will be convinced. You seem to hope it is true!

CAPTAIN. Yes, strangely enough; it must be, because the first supposition can't be proved; the latter can be.

LAURA. Have you any ground for your suspicions?

CAPTAIN. Yes, and no.

LAURA. I believe you want to prove me guilty, so that you can get rid of me and then have absolute control over the child. But you won't catch me in any such snare.

CAPTAIN. Do you think that I would want to be responsible for another man's child, if I were convinced of your guilt?

LAURA. No, I'm sure you wouldn't, and that's what makes me know you lied just now when you said that you would forgive me beforehand.

CAPTAIN [rises]. Laura, save me and my reason. You don't seem to understand what I say. If the child is not mine I have no control over her and don't want to have any, and that is precisely what you do want, isn't it? But perhaps you want even more—to have power over the child, but still have me to support you.

LAURA.   Power, yes! What has this whole life and death struggle been for but power?

CAPTAIN.   To me it has meant more. I do not believe in a hereafter; the child was my future life. That was my conception of immortality, and perhaps the only one that has any analogy in reality. If you take that away from me, you cut off my life.

LAURA.   Why didn't we separate in time?

CAPTAIN.   Because the child bound us together; but the link became a chain. And how did it happen; how? I have never thought about this, but now memories rise up accusingly, condemningly perhaps. We had been married two years, and had no children; you know why. I fell ill and lay at the point of death. During a conscious interval of the fever I heard voices out in the drawing-room. It was you and the lawyer talking about the fortune that I still possessed. He explained that you could inherit nothing because we had no children, and he asked you if you were expecting to become a mother. I did not hear your reply. I recovered and we had a child. Who is its father?

LAURA.   You.

CAPTAIN.   No, I am not. Here is a buried crime that begins to stink, and what a hellish crime! You women have been compassionate enough to free the black slaves, but you have kept the white ones. I have worked and slaved for you, your child, your mother, your servants; I have sacrificed promotion and career; I have endured torture, flagellation, sleeplessness, worry for your sake, until my hair has grown gray; and all that you might enjoy a life without care, and when you grew old, enjoy life over again in your child. I have borne everything without complaint, because I thought myself the father of your child. This is the commonest kind of theft, the most brutal slavery. I have had seventeen years of penal servitude and have been innocent. What can you give me in return for that?

LAURA.   Now you are quite mad.

CAPTAIN.   That is your hope!—And I see how you have labored to conceal your crime. I sympathized with you because I did not understand your grief. I have often lulled your evil conscience to rest when I thought I was driving away morbid thoughts. I have heard you cry out in your sleep and not wanted to listen. I remember now night before last—Bertha's birthday—it was between two and three in the morning, and I was sitting up reading; you shrieked, "Don't, don't!" as if someone were strangling you; I knocked on the wall—I didn't want to hear any more. I have had my suspicions for a long time but I did not dare to hear them confirmed. All this I have suffered for you. What will you do for me?

LAURA.   What can I do? I will swear by God and all I hold sacred that you are Bertha's father.

CAPTAIN.   What use is that when you have often said that a mother can and ought to commit any crime for her child? I implore you as a wounded man begs for a death-blow, to tell me all. Don't you see I'm as helpless as a child? Don't you hear me complaining as to a mother? Won't you forget that I am a man, that I am a soldier who can tame men and beasts with a word? Like a sick man I only ask for compassion. I lay down the tokens of my power and implore you to have mercy on my life.

.[LAURA *approaches him and lays her hand on his brow.*]

LAURA.   What! You are crying, man!

CAPTAIN.   Yes, I am crying although I am a man. But has not a man eyes? Has not a man hands, limbs, senses, thoughts, passions? Is he not fed with the same food, hurt by the same weapons, warmed and cooled by the same summer and winter as a woman? If you prick us do we not bleed? If you tickle us do we not laugh? And if you poison us, do we not die? Why shouldn't a man complain, a soldier weep? Because it is unmanly? Why is it unmanly?

LAURA.   Weep then, my child, as if you were with your mother once more. Do you remember when I first came into your life, I was like a second mother? Your great strong body needed nerves; you were a giant child that had either come too early into the world, or perhaps was not wanted at all.

CAPTAIN.   Yes, that's how it was. My father's and my mother's will was against my coming into the world, and consequently I was born without a will. I thought I was completing myself when you and I became one, and therefore you were allowed to rule, and I, the commander at the barracks and before the troops, became obedient to you, grew through you, looked up to you as to a more highly-gifted being, listened to you as if I had been your undeveloped child.

LAURA.   Yes, that's the way it was, and therefore I loved you as my child. But you know, you must have seen, when the nature of your feelings changed and you appeared as my lover that I blushed, and your embraces were joy that was followed by a remorseful conscience as if my blood were ashamed. The mother became the mistress. Ugh!

CAPTAIN.   I saw it, but I did not understand. I believed you despised me for my unmanliness, and I wanted to win you as a woman by being a man.

LAURA. Yes, but there was the mistake. The mother was your friend, you see, but the woman was your enemy, and love between the sexes is strife. Do not think that I gave myself; I did not give, but I took—what I wanted. But you had one advantage. I felt that, and I wanted you to feel it.

CAPTAIN. You always had the advantage. You could hypnotize me when I was wide awake, so that I neither saw nor heard, but merely obeyed; you could give me a raw potato and make me imagine it was a peach; you could force me to admire your foolish caprices as though they were strokes of genius. You could have influenced me to crime, yes, even to mean, paltry deeds. Because you lacked intelligence, instead of carrying out my ideas you acted on your own judgment. But when at last I awoke, I realized that my honor had been corrupted and I wanted to blot out the memory by a great deed, an achievement, a discovery, or an honorable suicide. I wanted to go to war, but was not permitted. It was then that I threw myself into science. And now when I was about to reach out my hand to gather in its fruits, you chop off my arm. Now I am dishonored and can live no longer, for a man cannot live without honor.

LAURA. But a woman?

CAPTAIN. Yes, for she has her children, which he has not. But, like the rest of mankind, we lived our lives unconscious as children, full of imagination, ideals, and illusions, and then we awoke; it was all over. But we awoke with our feet on the pillow, and he who waked us was himself a sleepwalker. When women grow old and cease to be women, they get beards on their chins; I wonder what men get when they grow old and cease to be men. Those who crowed were no longer cocks but capons, and the pullets answered their call, so that when we thought the sun was about to rise we found ourselves in the bright moon light amid ruins, just as in the good old times. It had only been a little morning slumber with wild dreams, and there was no awakening.

LAURA. Do you know, you should have been a poet!

CAPTAIN. Who knows.

LAURA. Now I am sleepy, so if you have any more fantastic visions keep them till tomorrow.

CAPTAIN. First, a word more about realities. Do you hate me?

LAURA. Yes, sometimes, when you are a man.

CAPTAIN. This is like race hatred. If it is true that we are descended from monkeys, at least it must be from two separate species. We are certainly not like one another, are we?

LAURA. What do you mean to say by all this?

CAPTAIN. I feel that one of us must go under in this struggle.

LAURA. Which?

CAPTAIN. The weaker, of course.

LAURA. And the stronger will be in the right?

CAPTAIN. Always, since he has the power.

LAURA. Then I am in the right.

CAPTAIN. Have you the power already then?

LAURA. Yes, and a legal power with which I shall put you under the control of a guardian.

CAPTAIN. Under a guardian?

LAURA. And then I shall educate my child without listening to your fantastic notions.

CAPTAIN. And who will pay for the education when I am no longer here?

LAURA. Your pension will pay for it.

CAPTAIN [*threateningly*]. How can you have me put under a guardian?

LAURA [*takes out a letter*]. With this letter of which an attested copy is in the hands of the board of lunacy.

CAPTAIN. What letter?

LAURA [*moving backward toward the door left*]. Yours! Your declaration to the doctor that you are insane. [*The* CAPTAIN *stares at her in silence.*] Now you have fulfilled your function as an unfortunately necessary father and breadwinner, you are not needed any longer and you must go. You must go, since you have realized that my intellect is as strong as my will, and since you will not stay and acknowledge it.

[*The* CAPTAIN *goes to the table, seizes the lighted lamp and hurls it at* LAURA, *who disappears backward through the door.*]

ACT III

Same scene. Another lamp on the table. The private door is barricaded with a chair.

LAURA [*to* NURSE].   Did he give you the keys?

NURSE.   Give them to me, no! God help me, but I took them from the master's clothes that Nöjd had out to brush.

LAURA.   Oh, Nöjd is on duty today?

NURSE.   Yes, Nöjd.

LAURA.   Give me the keys.

NURSE.   Yes, but this seems like downright stealing. Do you hear him walking up there, Ma'am? Back and forth, back and forth.

LAURA.   Is the door well barred?

NURSE.   Oh, yes, it's barred well enough!

LAURA.   Control your feelings, Margret. We must be calm if we are to be saved. [*Knock.*] Who is it?

NURSE [*opens door to hall.*]   It is Nöjd.

LAURA.   Let him come in.

NÖJD [*comes in*].   A message from the Colonel.

LAURA.   Give it to me. [*Reads*] Ah!—Nöjd, have you taken all the cartridges out of the guns and pouches?

NÖJD.   Yes, Ma'am.

LAURA.   Good, wait outside while I answer the Colonel's letter.

[NÖJD *goes.* LAURA *writes.*]

NURSE.   Listen. What in the world is he doing up there now?

LAURA.   Be quiet while I write.

[*The sound of sawing is heard.*]

NURSE [*half to herself*].   Oh, God have mercy on us all! Where will this end!

LAURA.   Here, give this to Nöjd. And my mother must not know anything about all this. Do you hear?

[NURSE *goes out,* LAURA *opens drawers in desk and takes out*

30

papers. The PASTOR *comes in, he takes a chair and sits near* LAURA *by the desk.*]

PASTOR.   Good evening, sister. I have been away all day, as you know, and only just got back. Terrible things have been happening here.

LAURA.   Yes, brother, never have I gone through such a night and such a day.

PASTOR.   I see that you are none the worse for it all.

LAURA.   No, God be praised, but think what might have happened!

PASTOR.   Tell me one thing, how did it begin? I have heard so many different versions.

LAURA.   It began with his wild idea of not being Bertha's father, and ended with his throwing the lighted lamp in my face.

PASTOR.   But this is dreadful! It is fully developed insanity. And what is to be done now?

LAURA.   We must try to prevent further violence and the doctor has sent to the hospital for a straitjacket. In the meantime I have sent a message to the Colonel, and I am now trying to straighten out the affairs of the household, which he has carried on in a most reprehensible manner.

PASTOR.   This is a deplorable story, but I have always expected something of the sort. Fire and powder must end in an explosion. What have you got in the drawer there?

LAURA [*has pulled out a drawer in the desk*].   Look, he has hidden everything here.

PASTOR [*looking into drawer*].   Good Heavens, here is your doll and here is your christening cap and Bertha's rattle; and your letters; and the locket. [*Wipes his eyes.*] After all he must have loved you very dearly, Laura. I never kept such things!

LAURA.   I believe he used to love me, but time—time changes so many things.

PASTOR.   What is that big paper? The receipt for a grave! Yes, better the grave than the lunatic asylum! Laura, tell me, are you blameless in all this?

LAURA.   I? Why should I be to blame because a man goes out of his mind?

PASTOR.   Well, well, I shan't say anything. After all, blood is thicker than water.

LAURA.   What do you dare to intimate?

PASTOR [*looking at her penetratingly*].   Now, listen!

LAURA.   Yes?

PASTOR.   You can hardly deny that it suits you pretty well to be able to educate your child as you wish?

LAURA.   I don't understand.

PASTOR.   How I admire you!

LAURA.   Me? H'm!

PASTOR.   And I am to become the guardian of that free-thinker! Do you know I have always looked on him as a weed in our garden. [LAURA *gives a short laugh, and then becomes suddenly serious.*]

LAURA.   And you dare say that to me—his wife?

PASTOR.   You are strong, Laura, incredibly strong. You are like a fox in a trap, you would rather gnaw off your own leg than let yourself be caught! Like a master thief—no accomplice, not even your own conscience. Look at yourself in the glass! You dare not!

LAURA.   I never use a looking glass!

PASTOR.   No, you dare not! Let me look at your hand. Not a tell-tale blood stain, not a trace of insidious poison! A little innocent murder that the law cannot reach, an unconscious crime—unconscious! What a splendid idea! Do you hear how he is working up there? Take care! If that man gets loose he will make short work of you.

LAURA.   You talk so much, you must have a bad conscience. Accuse me if you can!

PASTOR.   I cannot.

LAURA.   You see! You cannot, and therefore I am innocent. You take care of your ward, and I will take care of mine! Here's the doctor.

[DOCTOR *comes in.*]

LAURA [*rising*].   Good evening, Doctor. You at least will help me, won't you? But unfortunately there is not much that can be done. Do you hear how he is carrying on up there? Are you convinced now?

DOCTOR.   I am convinced that an act of violence has been committed, but the question now is whether the act of violence can be considered an outbreak of passion or madness.

PASTOR.   But apart from the actual outbreak, you must acknowledge that he has "fixed ideas."

DOCTOR.   I think that your ideas, Pastor, are much more fixed.

PASTOR.   My settled views about the highest things are——

DOCTOR.   We'll leave settled views out of this. Madam, it rests with you to decide whether your husband is guilty to the extent of imprisonment and fine or should be put in an asylum! How do you class his behavior?

LAURA.   I cannot answer that now.

DOCTOR.   That is to say you have no decided opinion as to what will be most advantageous to the interests of the family? What do you say, Pastor?

PASTOR. Well, there will be a scandal in either case. It is not easy to say.

LAURA. But if he is only sentenced to a fine for violence, he will be able to repeat the violence.

DOCTOR. And if he is sent to prison he will soon be out again. Therefore we consider it most advantageous for all parties that he should be immediately treated as insane. Where is the nurse?

LAURA. Why?

DOCTOR. She must put the straitjacket on the patient when I have talked to him and given the order! But not before. I have—the—garment out here. [*Goes out into the hall and returns with a large bundle.*] Please ask the nurse to come in here.

[LAURA *rings.*]

PASTOR. Dreadful! Dreadful!

[NURSE *comes in.*]

DOCTOR [*Takes out the straitjacket.*] I want you to pay attention to this. We want you to slip this jacket on the Captain, from behind, you understand, when I find it necessary to prevent another outbreak of violence. You notice it has very long sleeves to prevent his moving and they are to be tied at the back. Here are two straps that go through buckles which are afterwards fastened to the arm of a chair or the sofa or whatever is convenient. Will you do it?

NURSE. No, Doctor, I can't do that; I can't.

LAURA. Why don't you do it yourself, Doctor?

DOCTOR. Because the patient distrusts me. You, Madam, would seem to be the one to do it, but I fear he distrusts even you.

[LAURA's *face changes for an instant.*]

Perhaps you, Pastor——

PASTOR. No, I must ask to be excused.

[NÖJD *comes in.*]

LAURA. Have you delivered the message already?

NÖJD. Yes, Madam.

DOCTOR. Oh, is it you, Nöjd? You know the circumstances here; you know that the Captain is out of his mind and you must help us to take care of him.

NÖJD. If there is anything I can do for the Captain, you may be sure I will do it.

DOCTOR. You must put this jacket on him——

NURSE. No, he shan't touch him. Nöjd might hurt him. I would rather do it myself, very, very gently. But Nöjd can wait outside and help me if necessary. He can do that.

[*There is loud knocking on the private door.*]

DOCTOR.　There he is! Put the jacket under your shawl on the chair, and you must all go out for the time being and the Pastor and I will receive him, for that door will not hold out many minutes. Now go.

NURSE [*going out left*].　The Lord help us!

[LAURA *locks desk, then goes out left.* NÖJD *goes out back. After a moment the private door is forced open, with such violence that the lock is broken and the chair is thrown into the middle of the room. The* CAPTAIN *comes in with a pile of books under his arm, which he puts on the table.*]

CAPTAIN.　The whole thing is to be read here, in every book. So I wasn't out of my mind after all! Here it is in the Odyssey, book first, verse 215, page 6 of the Uppsala translation. It is Telemachus speaking to Athene. "My mother indeed maintains that he, Odysseus, is my father, but I myself know it not, for no man yet hath known his own origin." And this suspicion is harbored by Telemachus about Penelope, the most virtuous of women! Beautiful, eh? And here we have the prophet Ezekiel: "The fool saith; behold here is my father, but who can tell whose loins engendered him." That's quite clear! And what have we here? The History of Russian Literature by Merzlyakov. Alexander Pushkin, Russia's greatest poet, died of torture from the reports circulated about his wife's unfaithfulness rather than by the bullet in his breast from a duel. On his death-bed he swore she was innocent. Ass, ass! How could he swear to it? You see, I read my books. Ah, Jonas, are you here? and the doctor, naturally. Have you heard what I answered when an English lady complained about Irishmen who used to throw lighted lamps in their wives' faces? "God, what women," I cried. "Women," she gasped. "Yes, of course," I answered. "When things go so far that a man, a man who loved and worshipped a woman, takes a lighted lamp and throws it in her face, then one may know."

PASTOR.　Know what?

CAPTAIN.　Nothing. One never knows anything. One only believes. Isn't that true, Jonas? One believes and then one is saved! Yes, to be sure. No, I know that one can be damned by his faith. I know that.

DOCTOR.　Captain!

CAPTAIN.   Silence! I don't want to talk to you; I won't listen to you repeating their chatter in there, like a telephone! In there! You know! Look here, Jonas; do you believe that you are the father of your children? I remember that you had a tutor in your house who had a handsome face, and the people gossiped about him.

PASTOR.   Adolf, take care!

CAPTAIN.   Grope under your toupee and feel if there are not two bumps there. By my soul, I believe he turns pale! Yes, yes, they will talk; but, good Lord, they talk so much. Still we are a lot of ridiculous dupes, we married men. Isn't that true, Doctor? How was it with your marriage bed? Didn't you have a lieutenant in the house, eh? Wait a moment and I will make a guess—his name was—[*whispers in the* DOCTOR's *ear*]. You see he turns pale, too! Don't be disturbed. She is dead and buried and what is done can't be undone. I knew him well, by the way, and he is now—look at me, Doctor—No, straight in my eyes—a major in the cavalry! By God, if I don't believe he has horns, too.

DOCTOR [*tortured*].   Captain, won't you talk about something else?

CAPTAIN.   Do you see? He immediately wants to talk of something else when I mention horns.

PASTOR.   Do you know, Adolf, that you are insane?

CAPTAIN.   Yes; I know that well enough. But if I only had the handling of your illustrious brains for awhile I'd soon have you shut up, too! I am mad, but how did I become so? That doesn't concern you, and it doesn't concern anyone. But you want to talk of something else now. [*Takes the photograph album from the table.*] Good Lord, that is my child! Mine? We can never know. Do you know what we would have to do to make sure? First, one should marry to get the respect of society, then be divorced soon after and become lovers, and finally adopt the children. Then one would at least be sure that they were one's adopted children. Isn't that right? But how can all that help us now? What can keep me now that you have taken my conception of immortality from me, what use is science and philosophy to me when I have nothing to live for, what can I do with life when I am dishonored? I grafted my right arm, half my brain, half my marrow on another trunk, for I believed they would knit themselves together and grow into a more perfect tree, and then someone came with a knife and cut below the graft, and now I am only half a tree. But the other half goes on growing with my arm and half my brain, while I wither and die, for they were the best parts I gave away. Now I want to die. Do with me as you will. I am no more.

[*Buries his head on his arms on table. The* DOCTOR *whispers to the* PASTOR, *and they go out through the door left. Soon after* BERTHA *comes in.*]

BERTHA [*goes up to* CAPTAIN].   Are you ill, Father?

CAPTAIN [*looks up dazed*].   I?

BERTHA.   Do you know what you have done? Do you know that you threw the lamp at Mother?

CAPTAIN.   Did I?

BERTHA.   Yes, you did. Just think if she had been hurt.

CAPTAIN.   What would that have mattered?

BERTHA.   You are not my father when you talk like that.

CAPTAIN.   What do you say? Am I not your father? How do you know that? Who told you that? And who is your father, then? Who?

BERTHA.   Not you at any rate.

CAPTAIN.   Still not I? Who, then? Who? You seem to be well informed. Who told you? That I should live to see my child come and tell me to my face that I am not her father! But don't you know that you disgrace your mother when you say that? Don't you know that it is to her shame if it is so?

BERTHA.   Don't say anything bad about Mother; do you hear?

CAPTAIN.   No; you hold together, every one of you, against me! and you have always done so.

BERTHA.   Father!

CAPTAIN.   Don't use that word again!

BERTHA.   Father, Father!

CAPTAIN [*draws her to him*].   Bertha, dear, dear child, you are my child! Yes, Yes; it cannot be otherwise. It is so. The other was only sickly thoughts that come with the wind like pestilence and fever. Look at me that I may see my soul in your eyes!—But I see her soul, too! You have two souls and you love me with one and hate me with the other. But you must only love me! You must have only one soul, or you will never have peace, nor I either. You must have only one mind, which is the child of my mind and one will, which is my will.

BERTHA.   But I don't want to, I want to be myself.

CAPTAIN.   You must not. You see, I am a cannibal, and I want to eat you. Your mother wanted to eat me, but she was not allowed to. I am Saturn who ate his children because it had been prophesied that they would eat him. To eat or be eaten! That is the question. If I do not eat you, you will eat me, and you have already shown your teeth! But don't be frightened my dear child; I won't harm you.   [*Goes and takes a revolver from the wall.*]

BERTHA [*trying to escape*].   Help, Mother, help, he wants to kill me.

NURSE [*comes in*].   Mr. Adolf, what is it?

CAPTAIN [*examining revolver*].   Have you taken out the cartridges?

NURSE.   Yes, I put them away when I was tidying up, but sit down and be quiet and I'll get them out again!

[*She takes the* CAPTAIN *by the arm and gets him into a chair, into which he sinks feebly. Then she takes out the straitjacket and goes behind the chair.* BERTHA *slips out left.*]

NURSE.   Mr. Adolf, do you remember when you were my dear little boy and I tucked you in at night and used to repeat: "God who holds his children dear" to you, and do you remember how I used to get up in the night and give you a drink, how I would light the candle and tell you stories when you had bad dreams and couldn't sleep? Do you remember all that?

CAPTAIN.   Go on talking, Margret, it soothes my head so. Tell me some more.

NURSE.   O yes, but you must listen then! Do you remember when you took the big kitchen knife and wanted to cut out boats with it, and how I came in and had to get the knife away by fooling you? You were just a little child who didn't understand, so I had to fool you, for you didn't know that it was for your own good. "Give me that snake," I said, "or it will bite you!" and then you let go of the knife. [*Takes the revolver out of the* CAPTAIN*'s hand.*] And then when you had to be dressed and didn't want to, I had to coax you and say that you should have a coat of gold and be dressed like a prince. And then I took your little blouse that was just made of green wool and held it in front of you and said: "In with both arms," and then I said, "Now sit nice and still while I button it down the back." [*She puts the straitjacket on.*] And then I said, "Get up now, and walk across the floor like a good boy so I can see how it fits." [*She leads him to the sofa.*] And then I said, "Now you must go to bed."

CAPTAIN.   What did you say? Was I to go to bed when I was dressed— damnation! what have you done to me? [*Tries to get free.*] Ah! you cunning devil of a woman! Who would have thought you had so much wit. [*Lies down on sofa.*] Trapped, shorn, outwitted, and not to be able to die!

NURSE.   Forgive me, Mr. Adolf, forgive me, but I wanted to keep you from killing your child.

CAPTAIN.   Why didn't you let me? You say life is hell and death the kingdom of heaven, and children belong to heaven.

NURSE.   How do you know what comes after death?

CAPTAIN. That is the only thing we do know, but of life we know nothing! Oh, if one had only known from the beginning.

NURSE. Mr. Adolf, humble your hard heart and cry to God for mercy; it is not yet too late. It was not too late for the thief on the cross, when the Savior said, "Today shalt thou be with me in Paradise."

CAPTAIN. Are you croaking for a corpse already, you old crow?

[NURSE *takes a hymnbook out of her pocket.*]

CAPTAIN [*calls*]. Nöjd, is Nöjd out there?

[NÖJD *comes in.*]

CAPTAIN. Throw this woman out! She wants to suffocate me with her hymnbook. Throw her out of the window, or up the chimney, or anywhere.

NÖJD [*looks at* NURSE]. Heaven help you, Captain, but I can't do that, I can't. If it were only six men, but a woman!

CAPTAIN. Can't you manage one woman, eh?

NÖJD. Of course I can—but—well, you see, it's queer, but one never wants to lay hands on a woman.

CAPTAIN. Why not? Haven't they laid hands on me?

NÖJD. Yes, but I can't, Captain. It's just as if you asked me to strike the Pastor. It's second nature, like religion, I can't!

[LAURA *comes in, she motions* NÖJD *to go.*]

CAPTAIN. Omphale, Omphale! Now you play with the club while Hercules spins your wool.

LAURA [*goes to sofa*]. Adolf, look at me. Do you believe that I am your enemy?

CAPTAIN. Yes, I do. I believe that you are all my enemies! My mother was my enemy when she did not want to bring me into the world because I was to be born with pain, and she robbed my embryonic life of its nourishment, and made a weakling of me. My sister was my enemy when she taught me that I must be submissive to her. The first woman I embraced was my enemy, for she gave me ten years of illness in return for the love I gave her. My daughter became my enemy when she had to choose between me and you. And you, my wife, you have been my archenemy, because you never let up on me till I lay here lifeless.

LAURA. I don't know that I ever thought or even intended what you think I did. It may be that a dim desire to get rid of you as an obstacle lay at the bottom of it, and if you see any design in my behavior, it is possible that it existed, although I was unconscious of it. I have never thought how it all came about, but it is the result

of the course you yourself laid out, and before God and my conscience I feel that I am innocent, even if I am not. Your existence
has lain like a stone on my heart—lain so heavily that I tried to
shake off the oppressive burden. This is the truth, and if I have unconsciously struck you down, I ask your forgiveness.

CAPTAIN.   All that sounds plausible. But how does it help me? And
whose fault is it? Perhaps spiritual marriages! Formerly one married a wife, now, one enters into partnership with a business
woman, or goes to live with a friend—and then one ruins the part-
ner, and dishonors the friend!—What has become of love, healthy
sensuous love? It died in the transaction. And what is the result of
this love in shares, payable to the bearer without joint liability?
Who is the bearer when the crash comes? Who is the fleshly father of the spiritual child?

LAURA.   And as for your suspicions about the child, they are absolutely
groundless.

CAPTAIN.   That's just what makes it so horrible. If at least there were
any grounds for them, it would be something to get hold of, to
cling to. Now there are only shadows that hide themselves in the
bushes, and stick out their heads and grin; it is like fighting with
the air, or firing blank cartridges in a sham fight. A fatal reality
would have called forth resistance, stirred life and soul to action;
but now my thoughts dissolve into air, and my brain grinds a void
until it is on fire.—Put a pillow under my head, and throw something over me, I am cold. I am terribly cold!

[LAURA *takes her shawl and spreads it over him.* NURSE *goes to get
a pillow.*]

LAURA.   Give me your hand, friend.

CAPTAIN.   My hand! The hand that you have bound! Omphale!
Omphale!—But I feel your shawl against my mouth; it is as warm
and soft as your arm, and it smells of vanilla, like your hair when
you were young! Laura, when you were young, and we walked in
the birch woods, with the primroses and the thrushes—glorious,
glorious! Think how beautiful life was, and what it is now. You
didn't want to have it like this, nor did I, and yet it happened. Who
then rules over life?

LAURA.   God alone rules——

CAPTAIN.   The God of strife then! Or the Goddess perhaps, nowa-
days.—Take away the cat that is lying on me! Take it away!

[NURSE *brings in a pillow and takes the shawl away.*]

Give me my army coat!—Throw it over me! [NURSE *gets the coat and puts it over him.*] Ah, my rough lion skin that you wanted to take away from me! Omphale! Omphale! You cunning woman, champion of peace and contriver of man's disarmament. Wake, Hercules, before they take your club away from you! You would wile our armor from us too, and make believe that it is nothing but glittering finery. No, it was iron, let me tell you, before it ever glittered. In olden days the smith made the armor, now it is the needle woman. Omphale! Omphale! Rude strength has fallen before treacherous weakness.—Out on you, infernal woman, and damnation on your sex! [*He raises himself to spit but falls back on the sofa.*] What have you given me for a pillow, Margret? It is so hard, and so cold, so cold. Come and sit near me. There. May I put my head on your knee? So!—This is warm! Bend over me so that I can feel your breast! Oh, it is sweet to sleep against a woman's breast, a mother's, or a mistress's, but the mother's is sweetest.

LAURA.   Would you like to see your child, Adolf?

CAPTAIN.   My child? A man has no children, it is only woman who has children, and therefore the future is hers when we die childless. Oh, God, who holds his children dear!

NURSE.   Listen, he is praying to God.

CAPTAIN.   No, to you to put me to sleep, for I am tired, so tired. Good night, Margret, and blessed be you among women.

[*He raises himself, but falls with a cry on the nurse's lap.* LAURA *goes to left and calls the* DOCTOR, *who comes in with the* PASTOR.]

LAURA.   Help us, Doctor, if it isn't too late. Look, he has stopped breathing.

DOCTOR [*feels the* CAPTAIN'S *pulse*].   It is a stroke.

PASTOR.   Is he dead?

DOCTOR.   No, he may yet come back to life, but to what an awakening we cannot tell.

PASTOR.   "First death, and then the judgment."

DOCTOR.   No judgment, and no accusations. You who believe that a God shapes man's destiny must go to him about this.

NURSE.   Ah, Pastor, with his last breath he prayed to God.

PASTOR [*to* LAURA].   Is that true?

LAURA.   It is.

DOCTOR.   In that case, which I can understand as little as the cause of his illness, my skill is at an end. You try yours now, Pastor.

LAURA.   Is that all you have to say at this deathbed, Doctor?

DOCTOR.   That is all! I know no more. Let him speak who knows more.

[BERTHA *comes in from left and runs to her mother.*]

BERTHA. Mother, Mother!
LAURA. My child, my own child!
PASTOR. Amen.

CURTAIN.